Just a Customer

Just a Customer

John Lowrie

Marionette Books

© John Lowrie 1998

First published in 1998 by
Marionette Books
1 Hutton Close
South Church
Bishop Auckland
Durham

British Library Cataloguing in Publication Data.
A Catalogue record for this book is available
from the British Library.

ISBN 1 84039 009 3

Typeset by CBS, Felixstowe, Suffolk
Printed and bound by Antony Rowe Ltd, Chippenham

To my wife Louise

CHAPTER 1

Charlie Hammond wasn't having the best of days. He had just attended the funeral of one of his cronies. It had only been last Friday night they had all been playing dominoes in the White Swan, and now Fred Harding was gone forever. Charlie would probably not have felt so bad if they hadn't chosen 'Abide with Me' for the final hymn. It always upset him.

It was still early in the day, not quite lunch time, so Charlie decided to walk down the street to the local supermarket and do his weekly shopping. As he walked, his thoughts dwelled on the funeral. The tears had been near but he hadn't cried. Charlie could only remember having cried three times in his life, and of these only once at a funeral; that was for his wife Lilly. He hadn't cried at the funeral of his beloved sister or of his mother or father. He had cried at an air show that he had attended, must have been ten years ago now; there had been a lump in his throat when he had rubbed his hand over the smooth wheel of a Spitfire, but there had been no stopping the flow of tears when it flew slowly over the heads of the crowd. The third time he had cried was while in Fred Harding's house one Sunday afternoon. The television set was showing the test pilot doing taxiing trials with the new Concorde airliner. Unexpectedly the pilot had opened the throttles and Concorde had taken to the air. It was the most beautiful sight he had ever seen in his life and the tears had flowed down his cheeks.

Charlie pushed the supermarket door open and felt the welcome warm air on his face. Before starting his shopping he walked along the row of four tills. There were only two cashiers on duty and neither of them was Jos Edward's grand-daughter. She was the cashier that Charlie always made to. She was a cheeky little thing with a face to match. She always ribbed him with something or other, but always kept little bargains in a box under the till, things like burst bags of tea or sugar

1

just for coppers, and if there weren't any cracked eggs she would crack one for him and sell him half a dozen at half price. There was always a queue at her till even if there were others available. Charlie usually felt better after seeing her. She had been sacked before, after some old crow had complained of her ribbing, but they had lost so much business that the supermarket had been pleased to reinstate her.

Charlie changed his mind, decided to do his shopping another day and made to leave the shop. The manager approached him as he made for the door.

'Is there anything I can do to help, Sir?'

'I don't see May at her till today,' Charlie answered.

'Miss Edwards telephoned in this morning, Sir. She's a little off colour today but expects to be back with us tomorrow. But we are here to help you, we are all really keen to look after our customers in any way we can.'

'Thank you very much,' said Charlie as he left the supermarket.

CHAPTER 2

Charlie emerged from the supermarket, sat behind the glass in the bus shelter and enjoyed the heat of the sun through the glass. He pondered on the supermarket manager's parting words: 'We are all keen to look after our customers.' Customers, damned customers, that's all we are, each and every one of us from the day we are born till the day we're dead: these were the thoughts that were running through Charlie's head.

Charlie was eighty-three years old and lived in Barnforth, a town situated in the north-east of England. It was a typical town for that part of the country with two collieries close by, one of them now closed down, and a quarry producing sand and dolomite. There was a foundry and an industrial estate built just after the war and a brickworks. These were the main sources of employment. The main street in the town contained all the usual shops and services, which had seen steady changes over the years. The conversion of the town cinema to a supermarket had been the last major change.

Apart from five years spent in the Royal Air Force during the Second World War, this of course forced on him by conscription, Charlie had spent his entire life in Barnforth. When he looked back, something he was finding himself doing more and more these days, he realised that the time spent in the Royal Air Force had been the happiest, most satisfying, care-free days of his life.

Charlie's father had fought in the First World War, and apart from a few short leaves had spent the duration of the war in France. After the Armistice he had returned to his work as a foreman at the iron foundry, but his health had been ruined by gas attacks. Every winter he suffered terrible chest problems until the winter of 1926 when the chest problem turned to pneumonia and he had died. After his death, money became the big problem. Charlie's sister, who was two years older, was in

3

domestic work and his mother obtained work in the local laundry, but neither job was very well paid.

Charlie left school the following year and it was like all his birthdays and Christmases rolled into one. He had hated school. Being intimidated had always antagonised him and intimidation in those days was what the teachers thrived on, so Charlie's schooldays had been tough and it reflected in the education he had received – it was minimal.

Charlie's mother blamed the iron foundry for compounding the chest problems suffered by his father so she encouraged Charlie to seek employment elsewhere. Charlie sought and found work on a local farm. The farmer, Alec Brass, was a tyrant but he was fair – he was horrible to everyone! For the first year Charlie enjoyed the work, being given a variety of tasks to do, and to give Alec Brass his due, he did not expect Charlie to do too much heavy lifting such as humping sixteen-stone sacks of grain as the more mature men were expected to.

Charlie's second summer on the farm sickened him. He was promoted to a horseman and taught to plough. The farm boasted one of the largest fields in the district, about thirty acres, and that summer it had been left fallow to allow plenty of time for it to be prepared for a crop of winter wheat, sown about September/October. So while the rest of the farm men made hay, singled turnips and hoed potatoes, Charlie followed the two Shire horses up and down the massive field. Thirty-six days it took him to complete the field, during which time his boots were cobbled twice. His feet became so sore with blisters he could hardly walk and as the summer wore on the weather became hotter and the flies became a torment to both Charlie and the horses, making them fractious and difficult to handle. On top of that, Bess, the older horse, passed wind continuously, making the working conditions even worse.

It was a Saturday afternoon when Charlie finished the field and, doing as he had been told, he gave the horses a small bucket of water, just enough to take their thirst away, and a bite of the best hay. If they had been allowed into the pasture field after a spell of hard work and been allowed unrestricted access to the water trough they could have gone down with severe colic. While waiting for the horses to finish up their water and hay Charlie sat on an upturned bucket in an effort to ease his blistered, crippled feet. Alec Brass walked into the stable.

'Now then, Charlie,' he began with his thumbs stuck through his braces. 'I see you've finished the field, and not a bad job you've done, mind it's taken you longer than it should – a good ploughman should easy do an acre a day, but seeing as you're just starting I'll overlook it this time.'

Charlie just sat there, mouth open, looking at Alec Brass.

'On Monday morning I want you to get a good start, yoke the two horses onto the harrows and pull them twice over the same field, first time with the ploughing, second time across the ploughing. Then yoke the roller and pull that over the field, then put the plough back on and, starting at the same place as you did when you ploughed it last time, plough it again.'

Alec Brass reached over and put Charlie's pay into his hand – a ten shilling note, two half-crowns and a sixpenny piece. Charlie stood up.

'Mr Brass, that's my finish. I couldn't face that field again to save my life.'

'Now, Charlie, think careful on what you're saying – good, well paid jobs are bad to come by.'

'I'll take my chance,' said Charlie as he hobbled from the stable.

CHAPTER 3

Charlie emerged from the bus shelter and made his way slowly down the main street of the town. The sun was a little warmer by then, and this, coupled with the sadness he felt from the death of his friend, made the words of the supermarket manager looking after their customers the more poignant.

The first building Charlie came to was the old chapel. 'Yes, I have been a customer there,' thought Charlie. The chapel had over the years belonged to various religious groups, so many that Charlie had lost track of them. It was now disused, and in a dilapidated condition. It had been built of corrugated iron which was now rusty and practically bare of paint and it was an eyesore. The overgrown shrubs also contributed to its run down state.

Charlie cast his mind back to about 1960. A Preacher Jordan had come to the chapel one evening to give a religious talk. Charlie as usual wasn't in 'the good books' with his wife. There had been several arguments over his visits to the White Swan. She desperately wanted to go along and hear Preacher Jordan. To redeem himself, but under sufferance, he agreed to go along with her. Charlie had taken his religious education with some scepticism. He had heard all the usual bible stories, parables and, on his few forced visits to the Church, a few sermons. Larger than life characters, miracles and rising from the dead he just could not accept. Because the Church's teachings were a good way of life, however, essential if people were to live as a community, Charlie kept his thoughts to himself.

It was a wet, miserable night which had kept most of the community indoors by their firesides. Only about thirty people braved the elements to hear Preacher Jordan. The talk that the preacher gave was to stay in Charlie's mind forever. Preacher Jordan was a small man dressed in a conservative manner, not in the usual grey sombre colours associated

6

with pastors. His voice was quiet but penetrating, with an almost hypnotic quality to it; it forced the group of people to listen to him with all of their attention.

'Ladies and Gentlemen, I want to talk with you tonight about our Creator, for I am sure that you will agree with me that we do have a Creator – one of the few beliefs that all of the religions of the world are united in. Our Creator has not blessed us with enough brain power to understand the intricacies of his secrets; the best brains in the world have tried, but still don't understand any more than a five-year-old child does about the simplicity of life itself. We just do not know where we come from, how or why we are alive, or where we go to when we are dead. If we look around us and study nature in its simplest terms, we can establish a pattern of how our Creator works. He obviously hates waste of any kind. Dead vegetation provides nutrients for the next generation of plants. Dead animals provide food for another animal or insect; everything in nature whether it be plant, animal or insect fights hard for life and our Creator will give the strength needed for that fight. A small tree in a forest will reach its branches up to the light and push its roots far seeking the limited nutrients; the same tree standing alone without competition will be content to grow at a much slower pace. The same applies in the animal world. If the food supply is limited, they will develop the tenacity to survive. There is a definite, flexible pattern to life.

'Moving on, still trying to understand the same pattern, I don't believe that the man who spends his life on his knees in his church pleases our Creator any more than the man who spends his life down the mine retrieving the coal hidden under the earth so many thousands of years ago. I think that our Creator wants us to use the abilities that he has given us. The carpenter who excels himself with a beautiful piece of furniture, the engineer who builds bridges and railways through difficult countryside, the farmer who grows two blades of grass where only one grew before – I am sure all of these people please our Creator. All these things I have described and the many other things that people do in their everyday work should not be confused with the works done by our Creator. A man and wife who are good friends of mine, lovely people, very good at their school-teacher jobs but absolutely hopeless at anything practical, have to employ others to do the simplest tasks for them. Decorating, gardening, simple home maintenance are all beyond their capabilities. They spent a whole weekend trying to construct a rabbit hutch. They had the best of materials, and the best of tools but not one piece of wood was sawn straight or to the correct length; the nails that had not bent over had split the wood. Thankfully they have a sense of humour and were able to laugh at their futile efforts. Yet for all their ineptitude at the practical things they credit themselves with the production of three wonderful children, two girls and a boy, the most complex sophisticated engineering masterpieces in the universe. This is another small insight into the pattern our Creator works to.'

CHAPTER 4

Paster Jordan continued:
'I would like to tell you now a true story of an ordinary family, that I hope will give you an insight into this same pattern of life, how if we really need and want something the capability will be provided. Because I know this family and because they don't live too far away, and because perhaps a lot of you here tonight will know them too, there will be no names mentioned. The family that I speak of consists of a vicar, his wife and their son. They were good parents and wanted the best for their son, expecting him to achieve a university standard of education and so enter one of the professions, a doctor or a solicitor perhaps. Sadly this was not to be. As soon as he started school, the boy had problems with his health. The simple childhood diseases such as measles, whooping cough, chicken pox and mumps all took their toll. Illnesses which would normally be a week or two for most children always developed complications with the vicar's son and he would be away from school for months. It was always at a crucial period in his education, usually at the beginning of a new term. Then to cap it all he went down with diphtheria when he was eleven years old and in his scholarship class, giving him no chance whatever to further his education. He lay near to death for two weeks or more. That coupled with all the other diseases he had suffered left him puny and weak and with a severely weakened chest causing breathing problems.

'The vicar's wife had a sister who was married to a farmer, and they had two sons. His aunt, uncle and two cousins were good to the boy, inviting him to the farm on many occasions to help him recuperate from his ailments. He loved it on the farm, spending a lot of time in the woods on the north side. His cousins were several years older than him, strong, healthy and very hard working boys. He would have liked to help them but was unable to keep up with them.

9

'Eventually the vicar's son left school at fifteen years of age, a pathetic looking lad, intelligent but with his education far from completed. His mother begged him to take a sedentary job, but because of his poor education a job like this turned out to be impossible to find. About a fortnight after leaving school he surprised his parents by announcing that he had found a job. He was to be can-lad for a team of woodcutters. His parents were not pleased at his choice of employment but wisely said nothing, fully expecting him, because of his condition, to last only a few days in the job. His duties consisted of keeping the work cabin clean and feeding with scrap wood the pot-bellied stove which kept the cabin warm and was the means to heat the workmen's pies and the tin cans that held their tea.

'The can-lad enjoyed working in the woods, in the fresh air, and soon mastered his tasks. He soon found himself with time on his hands and began helping the woodcutters. The foreman was a kindly man, used to organising men, and he could see that the can-lad was not very strong, so he only allowed him to do light tasks such as trimming lighter branches and putting them in a pile ready to burn.

'The life-style suited the can-lad perfectly and because he wanted to be able to do the work, our Creator gave him the means to carry it out. His chest deepened, his shoulders opened out and broadened, muscles on his arms and legs developed, he gained weight and six inches in height! Very soon he was able to swing a full size felling axe and take the end of a seven foot cross-cut saw with the best of them. The foreman and the rest of the team were pleased to have him as part of the gang. The can-lad was now a woodcutter.

'The woodcutters worked on a piece-work system, and were paid so much a cubic foot for the timber they took from the forests. The money they earned was well above the average wage earned by similar workers. After a few years the woodcutter courted and married a young local girl. He was very lucky to win her affections as she was pretty, intelligent and in great demand from the other young men in the district.

'The woodcutter and his wife set up home in a modest house in the village where he had attended school. They were very happy together and soon had a son of their own. The wife was a natural thrifty person and very much appreciated how hard her husband worked to earn his money. She used all of her intellect and energy to make sure that none of it was wasted. They had enjoyable times sitting by the fire on an evening planning the major purchases that they were able to afford with the money she had saved.

'The woodcutter enjoyed a night out with his friends each week, always a Friday night and always in the village pub. He would have two or three pints of beer and a game of darts. His wife liked to go shopping in town with her sister on a Saturday afternoon, usually ending with "high tea" in a decent restaurant. The woodcutter was quite happy to stay at home taking care of their baby son. It was a well earned break for each of them.

'After a few years fortunes changed for the pair. Tragedy struck the farming uncle's family. One cousin was attacked by the bull and was mortally injured; the other cousin fearlessly went to his aid but sadly he too was killed. The tragic loss of the two boys so affected their father that after a short while he succumbed to a heart attack. Within a year the mother took a stroke and she too died, so within two short years the whole family was dead.

'When the woodcutter's aunt's will was studied it was found that the entire estate had been left to her nephew. The six hundred and fifty acre farm was fully paid for and stocked to the hilt with the best of stock. The land was in good heart and well manured. There was a range of first class agricultural implements and modern tractors, well able to do all the cultivation needed on such a large farm, whatever conditions prevailed. There was a good conscientious staff both on the farm and in the fine six-bedroom farmhouse. The farmhouse was tastefully furnished with the best of carpets and furniture. There was also a considerable amount of money in the bank. As it was such a complex estate it took the executors of the will several months to have probate granted, necessary before the farm could be handed over to the woodcutter. To keep the farm running while all this was taking place, the executors hired a farm manager.

'Eventually, when all was sorted out, the woodcutter and his wife and his son moved from the small house in the village to the grandeur of the farmhouse. The woodcutter was now a landowner.

'The landowner had to admit he didn't know much about farming, and he felt that he would like to enjoy his good fortune, take a rest from the hard work he had been used to and generally take things easy for a while. But there he made his first mistake. He asked the farm manager if he would take the job permanently. The farm manager was a rogue; the only things he would not steal were immovable.

'The landowner soon settled into his new lifestyle. It was all so easy. He didn't need to rise so early. He could afford to drink whisky daily at the best hotels instead of his usual two or three pints of beer at the pub once a week. He would spend sometimes two or three days a week at the race meetings, sometimes winning when he gambled, but mostly losing heavily.

'The landowner's wife also drifted into a much easier mode of living. She no longer had the same respect for her husband's money. She shopped without thought and allowed her household to be run by the hired help. The only thing they now did together was to visit the bank once a week where they both worked out their cash requirements. The landowner would write a cheque for that amount and always attended the same cashier who would smile sweetly and pass him the cash over the counter.

'All they had worked for while being a simple woodcutter and wife, our Creator slowly took from them. The man's strong muscular body gradually turned to fat; any exertion had him puffing like a broken-winded cuddy. His wife's sharp intellect left her, as did her thrift and sense of fairness. They became bored with themselves and boring to each other. Subconsciously each of them were looking for new partners in an effort to put something into their unfulfilled lives. Fortunately neither of them found anyone.

'The landowner's attitude to the farm suited the thieving manager right down to the ground, for all the running of the farm was left to him. He had complete control of the staff; he did all the ordering, all the buying and the selling; the landowner even trusted him to provide all the relevant information for his accountant and the bank. The manager had a free hand with everything on the farm. All the loyal members of staff were soon ousted and replaced with members of the manager's family and other cronies of his, who were only too willing to share in the spoils.

'The landowner's son, although still very young, had an interest in the farm but, because of what he might see, was very much discouraged by the staff from spending time there.

'One loyal farm worker was proving to be a thorn in the flesh of the manager. He had been sacked from his job but refused to leave the cottage that went with it. The manager applied, in his employer's name, for a court order to the local magistrate to have the worker evicted from his house. The worker was offered alternative accommodation which he refused, leaving the magistrate no alternative than to make an order for the court bailiff to remove him forcefully. Just two days before the court order was to take effect, the loyal farm worker asked his Union Secretary for assistance. Legally, in such a short time there wasn't anything the Union Secretary could do, but because he was an enterprising chap and the farm worker was such a popular, well liked man, he felt that he had to do something.

'The day before the eviction notice was to be carried out the Union Secretary travelled round all the farms in the district asking for assistance. On the morning of the planned eviction there were two bailiffs and a helper, plus a police constable, to make sure that there was no breach of the peace. Things started to go wrong for them however when they found that they were unable to approach the cottage with their vehicles. The roads to the farm were all blocked by "broken down" farm machinery. When they did eventually reach the cottage on foot they were met by about thirty burly farmers and farm workers all in the grounds of the cottage. It would have been a very brave bailiff who evicted the loyal farm worker that day.

'The court order was only valid for that one Saturday. After the weekend the case was back in front of the magistrates, who took a very dim view of what had happened. They issued another Order for two weeks later. Again there was not enough time for the Union Secretary to organise any legal assistance, but he knew that strong arm tactics would not work a second time. Only in the last few days was he able to think up a plan that might work. The Union's legal department had by now had time to study the case and their barrister had found that the magistrates had taken short cuts when dealing with the case. If the eviction notice could be thwarted once more, the barrister could ensure it would not be issued again.

'Two days before eviction day, the Union Secretary called on the loyal farm worker and his wife and put the plan to them that he had devised. They both grinned and readily agreed. When the Union

Secretary left he took with him a recent photograph of the loyal farm worker.

'The night before the eviction the loyal farm worker waited until it was nearly dark and left the cottage. He took the path over the fields and along the river bank and walked five miles to the main line railway station. From there he took the train to Edinburgh to stay with his sister until after the weekend.

'The second eviction day was also a Saturday, and this time the officials were ready for any eventuality. In the first van that arrived there were three bailiffs and three helpers, all obviously chosen for their heavy muscular build. In the second van there was a police inspector and ten constables, some of them borrowed from the neighbouring town ready to deal with any trouble that might ensue. The farm manager and some of his cronies were in the background to gloat on the farm worker's misfortune, and there was a joiner present ready to change the locks when the cottage was empty.

'The head bailiff knocked on the door with some force and it was instantly opened by the loyal farm worker's wife. She had a black shawl over her head, and by her side stood the Union Secretary, who was just a puny bespectacled little man. He had his arm round her shoulders. The head bailiff said his piece and handed the Court Order to the woman. Without a word, and with tears streaming down her face, she and the Union Secretary walked away from the open door to the far side of the tiny garden, distancing themselves from the bailiffs and the police.

'The inspector fleetingly caught the eye of the Union official; then he surveyed the rest of the scene. The horror of it dawned on him – he was Napoleon and this was his Waterloo. He could feel the scorn, the disdain, the contempt of the constables; it was radiating from them and was aimed entirely at him. Some of them were from the neighbouring town. He was near retiring age and during his whole career he had worked hard, been involved in the solutions of many complicated cases, had studied hard for his promotions and had earned the respect of his superiors and his subordinates. On this day all the good work he had done would be forgotten. This was his swan song. He would only be remembered for the events that were about to happen. Wherever policemen met this story would be retold and exaggerated. Every guffaw in the police canteen would be at his expense. He now knew why some men knocked their heads on stone walls and why ostriches buried their heads in the sand. Through clenched teeth he told the bailiffs to get on with it.

'They started with the kitchen furniture and soon the bailiff's helpers had a steady stream of pieces flowing from the cottage. Kitchen tables and chairs, a set of drawers with a cupboard on top, the floor covering; even the curtains were all stacked neatly outside the cottage. Then the stream stopped, One of the bailiffs hurried over to the inspector and told him to come with him quickly, that the man of the house was lying dead. The inspector entered the front room of the cottage where the curtains were drawn. In the darkened room was a fine oak coffin standing on a chromium plated trestle; in it was a wax bust in the exact likeness of the loyal farm worker. Made by theatrical friends of the Union Secretary, in the darkened room it looked only too real.

'The inspector gave instructions to the bailiffs to put back the furniture exactly as it had been. While they reverently carried out their task, the inspector approached the farm manager and his friends who stood dumbfounded as they watched the furniture being carried back inside. He told them to make themselves scarce and warned them that if he had a report of any of them being within a hundred yards of the cottage, he would think up charges and have them locked up for twenty years in solitary confinement on nothing but bread and water. They moved off quickly. A newspaper reporter had turned up to report on the eviction. He too was given a similar warning and was pleased to leave the scene.

'By then the bailiffs' job was finished. The cottage was restored to normal, the police constables were back in their van, the bailiffs and their helpers were in their vehicle and all were moving off down the road before they were settled in their seats. The embarrassed police inspector approached what he thought was the widow and apologised for what had happened; he left her a card with the telephone numbers of both his office and his home with instructions to call him if she had any harassment from any quarter. Then he too left.

'Neither the Union Secretary nor the loyal farm worker's wife had spoken a word. The crocodile tears dried up immediately, the black shawl was removed and, both grinning, they made a cup of tea with a little more than sugar and milk in it to help them over the ordeal. That night his friend came and took back the borrowed coffin.

'The farm manager did not dare approach the Court to apply for a new eviction order, for he didn't know why the previous one had been so abruptly terminated and was worried that the police inspector knew of his activities. Besides this, things were happening at the farm which were taking most of his attention.

'The first sign that the landowner had that anything was wrong was when the accountant returned all his books to him with a note saying that because of the unreliability of the information he was receiving he was no longer able to handle his account. The second indication was when he and his wife called at the bank for his usual weekly money. The pleasant cashier was embarrassed and told the landowner that she was unable to cash his cheque until he had a word with the bank manager. They were ushered into the bank manager's office, where they were told that there was some concern about the farm account, that a considerable overdraft had built up, and that if they didn't bring forward a business plan that would reduce the borrowings the bank would insist on the sale of a large part of the farm to cover their debts. With a nod from the bank manager the cashier then cashed their cheque.

'The landowner returned to the farm immediately and spoke to his manager, telling him what had happened at the bank. The farm manager was a plausible sort of fellow and told his employer not to worry about it, joking that there was no need to keep a dog and bark oneself. He added that he would chase up the farm merchant for a cheque he was owing and that there were cattle in the shed ready for market, assuring the landowner that the money from these sources would keep the bank happy until he was able to come up with the business plan they wanted. The landowner, having been brought up in a vicar's household and only ever having worked with hard-working honest woodmen, never having been in contact with wrongdoers accepted every word his farm manager said. In a word, he was gullible.

'Everything came to a head on the day the cattle were sent to the market. Late in the afternoon the cattle haulier's lorry came into the farmyard. It was travelling much too fast, and skidded to a stop just feet from the farmhouse door. The brakes of the lorry were still hissing air as the haulier, a massive man, well over six feet tall and solidly built, strode purposefully to the farmhouse door. The housekeeper had already left for home, so the haulier's loud knock was answered by the young maid, who announced his presence to the landowner.

'"Tell him to see my farm manager," was the answer.

'The haulier would not be put off and marched into the house accompanied by the protesting maid. He was furious and in broad local dialect he directed his anger at the landowner and his wife. He told them that he had been good friends with their uncle, aunt and cousins. He told them how hard they had worked to build the farm up to what it was. He called them "great useless taties" for allowing things to fall into the state that they were now in. He told them that he had collected fifteen fat cattle from the farm that morning. He picked up the telephone from the desk and quickly dialled a number that he was obviously used to ringing and asked to speak to the auctioneer. He then passed the telephone to the landowner and instructed him to ask how many he would be paid for. The answer was eleven.

'The haulier took the receiver from the landowner and instructed the auctioneer to hold on to the cheque for the four cattle they had discussed earlier and wait until the situation was resolved. The landowner reached for his second line of defence – the whisky bottle; he poured good measures into two glasses and pushed one over the desk to the haulier, who in a rage hurled both bottle and glasses into the empty stone fireplace where they smashed to pieces. He continued to rate the landowner who was told in no uncertain language to "pull himself together", to "take hold of himself" and to "open his eyes" to what Ali Baba and his forty thieves in the guise of his manager and workers were doing to him.

'The haulier made to storm from the room, but before he reached the door he turned and faced the landowner again. He told him to talk to the loyal farm worker who knew much more than him as to what was happening on the farm, and then to call in the police. With that he left, his lorry leaving a cloud of dust as it left the farmyard.

'All his advice had been punctuated with some very colourful language.

'The landowner and his wife were dumbfounded. They were angry that they had been scolded and humiliated by the cattle haulier. The realisation of what had happened on the farm upset their emotions far more. For a while they were unable to speak and could only stand there and look at each other. Later that evening they had their first real talk for years, in fact since right back when the man had been a woodcutter. They planned their course of action well into the night, deciding that their first move would be to speak to the loyal farm worker.

'The landowner was embarrassed calling on his loyal employee the following morning, owing to what had happened previously, but he need not have worried as the man was delighted to have the opportunity to help and suggested a walk round the farm. The whole extent of what had been happening became apparent to him as they looked around the fields, some of which he was ashamed to admit he had not set foot in since inheriting the farm. Not only had the farm manager and his cronies been helping themselves to a big percentage of the farm produce, they had also been selling the pedigree seed grain and expensive artificial fertilisers to other unscrupulous farmers. Grain only suitable for poultry food had been drilled on the farm and this coupled with the lack of fertiliser meant the crops were a disgrace. This could clearly be seen when comparison was made with neighbours' crops. The canker had also spread into the farmhouse, right under their noses. A proportion of the coal for heating and meat for the table had all been delivered to different addresses.

'With all the evidence before them the police had no difficulty obtaining convictions for all who had been implicated in the thieving, but the monies had been shared out and spent without hope of it ever being returned. Thanks to the livestock haulier, the landowner was able to recover the money for the four cattle but that was a small percentage of all that the farm manager and his friends had stolen in four years.

'The landowner felt such a fool for being so blind to what had been going on. He felt dreadful at how badly he had let down his uncle, aunt and cousins, and realised the only way to make amends would be to do the farming himself.

'The landowner was now a farmer. He was starting with a clean sheet, his thieving staff all sacked, but with no idea where to start. Fortunately for him the loyal farm worker agreed to work with him, and as he had been his uncle's right hand man he knew what had to be done. He was however no longer a young man and the bulk of the work had to fall on the farmer's shoulders.

'Life for the farmer's wife changed too; she was left with only one honest young girl to help with the running of the farmhouse. As the farmer was so busy seeing to the farm, the financial mess at the bank and at the accountants had to be put into her hands to resolve.

'When the accountants heard of what had happened on the farm, they agreed to take on the farm accounts again, but only on condition that she came to the office on a regular basis to keep them right up to date as to what was happening. The bank were more difficult to convince that a genuine effort was being made. Luckily the farmland had increased in value, so, with certain provisos, they were willing to increase the overdraft facilities to allow the farmer and his wife to stay in business. With this new challenge in her life, it was just what was needed to bring back her old instincts. The pressure they were under helped her to bloom again. The farmer didn't find it so easy; the sheer physical effort tried him to his utmost. It was as if our Creator was saying, "I made it easy for you the last time you needed strength and fitness. This time you do most of it yourself." Blisters formed on his hands and burst; the pain was horrendous. His former dependence on whisky brought out embarrassing sweats, and with every effort he made, he had to fight for breath. The heavy farm boots he was forced to wear skinned his toes and heels, making even more pain to bear. To frustrate him, the quality hand tools his uncle had left, which would have made life a lot easier, had been sold by the thieves. All farming machines have replaceable wearing parts, and if they are not replaced when worn down, the machines are soon ruined. This is what had happened to the farmer's best machines. Oh yes, he had bought these parts but they had never been fitted; they had been sold to other less than honest farmers.

'It was a terrible uphill struggle for the man. He soon learned a lot about farming, and one of the first discoveries was that you only got one chance to do each major task. If you were late, the season was missed, with dire results. He dreaded hearing the loyal farm worker's favourite phrase, "We'll have to make sharp."

'Gradually things improved. The farmer's wife had the financial side of the business under control, and she was in full charge of her household. She made sure that the farmer's diet was correct which helped him lose a lot of the unnecessary weight he was carrying. His son, although too young to be any real help, spent a lot of time with him on the farm. The aptitude he showed gave the farmer a lot of pleasure and a little respite from his suffering. It took two years before there was any semblance of order on the farm. He was able eventually to replace many of the stolen articles. He was learning his new trade quickly, and was now a shrewd farmer, thanks to the direction shown him by his loyal farm worker. By now he could have afforded extra help, but because of his recent experience, he was reluctant to do so. He chose to continue using seasonal contractual help, which he had relied on since the dismissal of his farm manager. The livestock haulier came back to apologise for his outburst, and the farmer duly thanked him for his concern over the farm. They shook hands, became friends, and resumed their business together. The farm was by no means up to the standard it had been when under his uncle's ownership, but it was intact, healthy, and on the up.

'I hope this story, which is indeed true, will show you how our Creator will help us to solve the problems that life throws at us. If we give our all, both mentally and physically, into whatever we want to do, our Creator will do His part and ensure that the wherewithal is provided, enabling us to gain satisfaction from the life He has given us.'

There had been utter silence all the time Pastor Jordon was speaking and even after he had sat down, there were only murmurings amongst his audience. One of the chapel officials announced that there would be a short break and that the ladies of the Chapel would provide tea and scones. After the break Pastor Jordon would address them again.

Charlie felt slightly out of place, not being a regular chapel-goer. He was unable to join into any of the conversational groups that formed. The time had moved round to eight thirty, when usually Charlie's character would show itself and he would be pressing Lilly to return home, to allow time for his nightly visit to the White Swan for a couple of glasses of beer and a game of dominoes. This night however he found himself enthralled with Pastor Jordon; he had really enjoyed listening to the story, though try as he might, he could not place the farming family that had been the centre of Pastor Jordon's talk. He contented himself with the cup of tea and scone, and waited patiently for the pastor to carry on with his discourse.

'I would like to carry on, if I may, on much the same lines as earlier, to take a simple view of our Creator's pattern of thinking. As I said before, we haven't the ability to understand the deeper complexities of life. Theologists the world over have spent life-times studying these things, and at the end of it all they are unable to answer the simple question of any five-year-old, "Where do we come from?"

'Let us take a look at one of his simpler creations, a river. You will argue with me that a river is not a life form, but let us look closer. It is born in the hills, and its life starts as ours, tumbling and skipping down the slopes, gaining strength, looking, as we look, for its course in life. When it reaches the lower ground, like us in middle life it slows, widens, deepens, and develops character. Like us it is expected to work. We harness it as we would a carthorse, but heaven help those who do not respect it, for as we have all seen, like a carthorse not respected, it can kill. In some countries of the world, the river is the sole means of support for whole communities, who use it for hygiene, for irrigation for their crops, for hydro-electricity for their light and heat, for food in the form of fish, even for their recreation. It is in fact so respected by some, that it is looked upon as holy, and is actually worshipped, proving that the river, in many people's eyes, is alive. Is there any wonder that all the major cities of the world are built on the banks of the river?

'In our part of the world, we use the river in a different way. It is expected to work in the same manner as we work, carrying the products, and disposing of the wastes of collieries, quarries, farms and iron works. It works for our power stations, carrying coal to them in barges, cooling them in their massive towers. We build all manner of ships on the rivers: war ships to protect our shores; tankers to move oil round the world; refrigerated ships, so that fresh meat, fruit and vegetables can be traded; fishing boats to brave the seas and harvest the oceans. Our rivers play their part in all this. Docks are always in the river mouth, where world trade originates.

'In all this activity the river, like us, keeps its character, sometimes angry, sometimes tranquil; also like us it mirrors its environment. In industrial areas it is sombre and grey, in the countryside it is bright and clear, much happier looking.

'As the river nears the end of its life, how I wish I could say, with any degree of certainty, that it resembles the end of our lives. The river returns to whence it came, back into the bosom of the ocean, no matter what has happened to it in its lifetime, how filthy we have made it, with our factory wastes and sewage. In the ocean it is sterilised with salt, repurified by condensation, and carried back to the mountains by the elements to start its life anew, maybe even to follow the same course. Whichever way we look at it, the river does have a life, and we know that it is reborn over and over again.

'I've spoken to you tonight, not to preach, but to try and leave you with a little something to think on. I want you to ask yourselves questions on how our Creator works, and I want to ask you to take just an hour each week, and sit, preferably in your Chapel, on a Sunday, and give Him your full thoughts, and attention. Thank you, ladies and gentlemen, for listening to me. I will now ask Mr White to close our meeting with a hymn, and a short prayer.'

Charlie had long since forgotten the hymn and the prayer, but he would remember forever Preacher Jordon's talk. Charlie looked again at the dilapidated chapel, and said to himself, 'Yes, I've been a customer there.'

CHAPTER 5

Contrary to Alec Brass's words, Charlie had no difficulty finding another job. The foundry where his father had worked, and been so well thought of, was only too pleased to have Charlie on the pay-roll. The foreman over the four-man gang that Charlie was assigned to, Harry Collins, had been a particular friend of Charlie's father, and was happy to welcome Charlie into his gang.

The work was entirely different from that on the farm. The main difference was that long hours on the farm with only your own company tended to magnify any problems on your mind, whereas at the foundry there was conversation, and someone always ready to make a joke out of a situation, preventing any depression building up. Hence Charlie became a much more sociable person. Even so, sometimes he missed the open spaces, the fresh air, and the opportunity to lose himself in his thoughts, as occasionally happened when he had worked on the farm.

It was a perfect time for Charlie to take up the foundry work. The firm had full order books and were looking for as much production as possible. The men were paid a weekly wage, plus a production bonus which could sometimes double their wages, making them some of the best paid men in the area. For these rewards the men were only too keen to give of their best, and put great effort into their work. Charlie found it hard, at first, to keep up with his new workmates, but soon the muscles needed for this type of work developed and he became used to the heat; eventually he felt that he was a useful member of the work-gang. The extra money made a vast difference to his home life. He was able to contribute more to the household and make life much easier for his mother, who could give up her job at the laundry. She showed her appreciation in ways that boosted Charlie's confidence. The main meal time was now linked to the time his shift at work ended; his clothes were mended, washed and ironed regularly. She even sought his advice on household problems, though Charlie knew she didn't need it. He overheard her gossiping to a neighbour one evening and her glowing picture of him left him red-faced. These were just minor things, but they did wonders for his morale and general well being.

The environment in the foundry however was more difficult. It was always so hot, and the burning coal and coke gave off choking fumes that made breathing unpleasant. The management recognised these problems and gave the men a daily allowance for liquid, to alleviate the loss of body fluids caused by excessive sweating, and to relieve the burning in the throat caused by the fumes. The liquid was intended to be milk, but most of the men chose beer. There was a public house just outside the foundry gate, appropriately called 'The Foundry'. The landlord had a special licence, allowing him to open to suit the foundry shifts. Every day Charlie would have a pint of beer half way through his shift and another when the shift was over. For Charlie the taste for beer was established, and he had enjoyed his pint ever since.

Some of the biggest shareholders in the foundry were Jewish. As Saturday was their Sabbath, only the most pressing tasks were undertaken on that day, consequently Charlie and his mates found themselves with most Saturdays free. His favourite day out was to meet up with a couple of his work mates, of about the same age as himself, and catch the ten o'clock train into Newcastle. It was about twenty minutes journey time. They would look around the shops and the markets and listen to the spiel of the barrow boys. At lunchtime they would make their way down to the riverside, to the Three Bells, where they would have a 'pie and a pint'. They would then walk to the football ground. The match kicked off at three o'clock, but they needed to be there a good half hour before that, to allow time to queue and to find a good place to stand. Charlie always enjoyed watching professionals play. Usually in every match there would be two or three outstanding players whose skills he really appreciated. Strangely, it didn't bother him whether the home or the away team won. It was the high standard of football he enjoyed. The game usually finished about twenty to five, when they would hurry from the ground to a café by the railway station and order fish and chips, which they would eat in a hurry. Then on to a billiard hall which had fourteen tables on two floors. They would hire a table for an hour and enjoy a game. After that they would seek out a good variety show at one of their three favourite theatres, one where they could have a good laugh. These shows usually went on till about ten or quarter past, and the last train home was twenty minutes to eleven. It allowed plenty of time for a steady walk to the station. Charlie was always home around ten past eleven, after a wonderful day out. His mother was always waiting for him with the kettle on the boil, ready to make him a pot of tea. She would tease him by saying, 'I don't know what's to happen to you, our Charlie, out again the full clock round.' Charlie had a laugh at the mock severity in her voice.

The enthusiasm for Charlie's days at Newcastle was permanently blunted after an incident one Saturday afternoon. The home team were to play one of the big London clubs, a match that was crucial to both teams, one of the last matches to determine their position in the League. It had been well publicised in the newspapers, and there was tremendous interest in it. To make sure of a good position on the terraces, Charlie and his two mates made to the Three Bells an hour early for their 'pie and a pint', then went straight up to the football ground. Everyone else however seemed to have had the same idea. The nearer they got to the ground, the more chaotic it became. There were so many people on the street that traffic was halted completely and the crush of people even shattered two shop windows. In the confusion Charlie became separated from his two mates. All he could do was to flow along with the crowd, till he eventually found himself through the turnstile and into the ground. Finally he reached the terraces, which were already three quarters full, and the crowd still pouring in.

Charlie took up a position behind one of the crush barriers and was soon hemmed in by the volume of the crowd. By the time it came to the kick off, the pressure on Charlie was frightening. The weight on his midriff made him grasp the crush barrier with both hands and lower his body, so that he could transfer his strength to his fore-arms, in an effort to relieve his discomfort. From this position, all Charlie could see was a strip of the football field about a yard wide, at the far side of the pitch. Children in the crowd were being passed hand over hand by the adults to the front, to save them from the crush. There were so many of them that they were crowded right up to the touch lines. The linesmen had to run on the actual playing pitch in order to do their jobs.

From the position Charlie was in, he could see nothing of the match, and only saw the ball when it was over head high. He found himself dreading any exciting move on the part of either side. The resulting surge sapped his strength, for he had to take the full weight of the crowd on his ribs. As his strength ebbed, panic gripped him; he felt he was going to be crushed to death.

Just in time for Charlie the half time whistle was blown and several of the spectators behind him moved out of the crowd, some to use the toilets, others to seek refreshments. The pressure eased slightly and Charlie, using the last of his power, pulled himself to one side and was free of the barrier that was causing him so much anguish. He threaded himself painfully through the crowd to the exit, and back onto the street.

Even though it was a warm sunny day, in Charlie's distressed eyes everything appeared grey. He made his way down the same street as he had come, passing the workmen erecting shuttering over the shattered shop windows, and when he felt that he couldn't walk any further, he sat down on a low wall. It was a wide pavement, directly opposite a bus stop. He had only been there for a few minutes when a mother and daughter came to wait for the bus. The mother, seeing Charlie, walked halfway over the pavement, and was looking hard at him.

The daughter called to her mother, in what was a half shout, 'Leave him be, Ma, ya can see he's the worse for drink.'

The mother bawled back at her, 'Shut ya bliddy gob, our Bessie. Bliddy ignorant, that's your trouble.'

'Oh no,' thought Charlie, 'I don't need this.'

The mother sat down on the wall beside him and, in a completely different temperament, put a huge arm tenderly round his shoulders, saying 'What's a marra, bonnie lad, ya lucken arfull badly.'

'I've been to the match, I've had to come out, I've nearly had the life squashed out of me.'

She said, 'Luk, there's a hospital, just a few hundred yards up the street, if ya want, ah'll get the bus after this un and ah'l tak ya up, th're very good, th'ul hev a luk at ya.'

'Thanks all the same, but I've two mates still in there. I'm going to meet them in the café by the station, then I'm going home to bed.'

'All right then, bonnie lad, as lang as yu'll be weel enough.'

At this point the bus arrived and mother and daughter boarded it, arm in arm. The sympathy shown by the mother comforted Charlie a little. He rose from his seat on the wall and made his way painfully towards the railway station, with the intention of catching an early train home. He entered the waiting room and found a comfortable seat, where he could think more clearly. He found that by keeping his breathing very shallow, he could control the terrible pain in his chest. He knew his two mates would come to the café over the road when the match was finished, and that they would be concerned if they couldn't find him, so decided that when the time came, he would go there and wait for them. He could see the station clock through the waiting room window. When it showed four thirty, he crossed the road to the café, bought a cup of tea, and sat by the window. Ten minutes later, an older man came into the café, bought a cup of tea, and sat at the same table as Charlie. He was a football fan whom Charlie and his mates often met after a game.

He was very talkative, and as soon as he sat down he said to Charlie, 'That was some crowd at the match to-day, young fellow, eh! Mind, ah thought if it hadn't been for our goalie, we could have been two or three goals down in the first half. We were half asleep, to let them have their chances. Mind, we wakened up in the second half, but didn't their left back play a blinder! If it hadn't been for him, ah think we could have had the result, but by and large, I think nought each was a fair result.'

'Aye,' said Charlie.

'Aye,' said the other man. With that, he hurried from the café and boarded a tram-car.

A few minutes later Charlie's two mates walked in and while they were waiting for their fish and chips, one of them said, 'What did you think of the match, Charlie?'

'That was some crowd, eh! Mind, ah thought if it hadn't been for our goalie, we could have been two or three goals down in the first half; we were half asleep, to let them have their chances. Mind, we wakened up in the second half, but didn't their left back play a blinder! If it hadn't been for him, ah think we could have had the result, but by and large, on the whole, ah think nought each was a fair result.'

'Aye,' said Charlie's mates in unison.

'Aye,' said Charlie.

Although in pain, Charlie accompanied his mates to the billiard hall, played for an hour, and carried on to the theatre. It was a good variety show with an exceptional singer, but the star of the show was a comedian. He was really funny and Charlie would have loved to join his mates in a good belly laugh. The pain in his ribs wouldn't allow it, however. Luckily the show finished quite early, allowing them plenty of time to walk to the station for the train home.

Charlie's mother wasn't her usual self when welcoming him home after his day out.

'I'm awfully worried about our Hannah, Charlie; a neighbour from up the street had to bring her home to-day. Seemingly she fainted at the bus stop, and it was ages before she came round. You know, when she did get home and I put her to bed, Charlie, there's not a picking on her; she is as weak as a kitten. I'm having the doctor to her on Monday, Charlie; I'm worried there's something serious wrong with her.'

All the time his mother was talking, it was as if she was mechanical, making Charlie his mug of tea while on her mind was his sister Hannah. Charlie was ready for bed before she got round to asking how his day had been. Not wanting to put any more worries on her shoulders he didn't mention the troubles he had had at the match. He said, 'There was some crowd at the game to-day, mother. Mind, ah thought if it hadn't been for our goalie, we could have been two or three goals down in the first half . . .'

'Aye,' said his mother.

'Aye,' said Charlie.

The following morning, after a disturbed night's sleep owing to the pain in his ribs every time he turned in bed, Charlie examined his midriff and was alarmed by the severe bruising round his ribcage: a large area was practically black. He knew the family doctor, a Scot by the name of Gordon, held a surgery on a Sunday morning. On the pretence of taking a Sunday morning stroll, he took himself to the surgery. Because of Charlie's father's long health problems, Dr Gordon had been a regular visitor to Charlie's home, so he knew him well. The doctor had a very quick wit, and he liked to know all the goings on, and all the local gossip.

He greeted Charlie with the words, 'It's not often I see you in here, young Charlie. What can I do for you, and is there anything fresh in

28

your street?'

'Nothing fresh, Doctor, but our Hannah had a bit of a bad turn yesterday; our Ma'll be sending for you tomorrow, if she's no better. Will you not mention I've been in, I don't want to worry her.'

'Sure, Charlie, that's very thoughtful of you. Now, what's the problem?'

'I went to the match yesterday, and I was crushed against the barrier.' Charlie put his hand on his ribs, to indicate where he was hurting.

'Take your shirt off, Charlie, and let me have a look.'

Charlie slowly removed his shirt, and when the doctor saw the extent of his injuries, he whistled through his teeth, and said, 'You've certainly been crushed, Charlie, but maybe its ya heed ah should be looking at, for getting into such a situation, eh?'

'Oh, very funny, Doctor.' Charlie tried to laugh, but it hurt too much. Dr Gordon felt round Charlie's chest till he came to the most painful part, and pressed his fingers into his ribs. Charlie winced with pain.

'Hm,' said the doctor, 'You've got at least one, maybe two, cracked ribs, and some very severe bruising. You'll be pleased to know you've no internal damage. You are going to have a painful week or two, because all I can do for you is to bind the ribs with a strong bandage, just to give a little support while they heal.'

Doctor Gordon took a bandage from the shelf and, to keep the conversation going, said, 'What did you think of the match, anyway?'

'There was some crowd at the match, Doctor. Mind, I think if it hadn't been for our goalie, we could have been two or three goals down in the first half . . .'

'Aye,' said the doctor.

'Aye,' said Charlie.

CHAPTER 6

Charlie had wandered about fifty yards down the High Street, and found himself gazing at a sink at the roadside. It was partially blocked and a small puddle had formed round it. He grinned as he recalled how Fred Harding, the friend whose funeral he had just attended, had walked with Charlie past this same spot, just two weeks ago. They had been at the White Swan, and perhaps had one more than usual. It had been raining heavily, and the road and the pavement were flooded halfway over. It had stopped raining before they left the pub. It was the rain that had been responsible for them having the extra pint; they had been ready to leave, but had turned back because of it.

It was one of those nights when the moon looked enormous. As they approached the flooded part of the road, there was a double deck bus coming. They held back, to avoid being splashed by the bus wheels. When the traffic was clear, they hurried past the flooded section. When safely over, Charlie found he was alone. Fred had stopped right in the middle of the water.

Charlie called, 'Come on, Fred, hurry up; if any more traffic comes you'll be soaked.'

'Come back here and see, Charlie!'

Thinking it was something important, Charlie reluctantly returned to Fred's side.

'What's the matter, why have you stopped?'

Fred was gazing at the reflection of the enormous moon. 'Charlie, if I was going to the moon, this is the night I'd set off. It's so close you could see your way all the way there.'

Charlie swore at him, and told him not to be so daft and to get a move on.

It was too late, two clowns in a sports car saw the situation, speeded up, drove through the flood, and soaked them right up to the knees. For all Charlie was grinning, it was with great sadness that he remembered the incident.

CHAPTER 7

Charlie found himself looking at the small single-window shop, which was directly opposite the partially blocked drain. The shop was called MBC Electronics, and it sold new and used washing machines, vacuum cleaners, and other household electrical gadgets. It also offered a repair service. It was plain to see that it had been painted by an amateur, Charlie was the first to admit; he was by no means an expert on colour co-ordination, but even to him, the colours clashed. Garish would be a simple way to describe it.

It was a very different shop that Charlie remembered, and no matter how brightly it was painted, in his memory it would always be grey. It had belonged to Mr Jeremiah Wild, and had sold wallpaper, paint and other home decorating requirements. To all outside appearances Jeremiah Wild was a pillar of society. He looked after his shop in business hours, and divided his spare time between his family and his church. He had married, late in life, a meek, quiet woman who wouldn't say boo to a goose. They had a daughter, just a few months older than Charlie, who had inherited the same characteristics as her mother. She was in the same class at school as Charlie. Jeremiah Wild was verger at the church. Because of his long term association with it and his forceful ways, he held more sway than the vicars who had the misfortune to be assigned to the Parish. Charlie knew him to be a vile, rotten, swine of a man.

Charlie's detestation of Jeremiah Wild had began when Charlie was just a child.

Growing up in the nineteen twenties hadn't been easy. With wages so low and conditions so difficult, parents found it hard enough to provide food, clothing and shoes, without having energy left to entertain their offspring. Children of Charlie's age were expected to occupy themselves.

At the end of Pear Street, two streets from Charlie's home, two semi-detached houses had been burned down, with the tragic loss of four lives. This had happened long before Charlie's time and, in the words of the proverb, 'it's an ill wind that does nobody any good', for when the rubble was cleared, the site of the two houses and their gardens had been abandoned and formed the ideal playground for all the youngsters in the neighbourhood.

From the age of five or six years old, Charlie's leisure time had been spent at this playground. In the main it was a happy place, but it was also the place where young fellows settled their differences. These fights didn't usually last long. The first one to bleed, cry, or be knocked down was the loser. One of these fights did stand out in Charlie's memory. Sandy Franklin and Eddie Smith both worked at the colliery, and were strong young men. They fought for an hour, knocking 'seven bells' out of one another. It was for who should have Greta Young as his sweetheart. They had each been so badly beaten that they had had to be taken home by their respective friends. It turned out to be all for nothing. Greta had married her cousin the previous week.

The time Charlie had spent in this make-shift playground had left him with a lot of happy memories. The main pastime for the boys was football. Given the limited room at the playground, it wasn't possible to have a proper pitch, so they played 'three goals in'. The game only needed one goal, which consisted of two broom shanks. The rules were simple: the first one to score three goals had the honour of being goalkeeper, till someone else scored three, then he took over. The ball was the most important part of the game and acquiring one was often a problem. Charlie had seen the game played with balls of all variations, from beach balls to tennis balls. The advantages of the game were that any number could play, and that anyone could join in or drop out, as the mood took them. If anyone was called for a meal or to run a message, the game wasn't spoiled. The game could also start and finish whenever it was convenient. One game could last two or three hours, with maybe an entirely different set of players at the end of the game than had been in at the start. It was a game that provided valuable training for the game proper, as they learnt to defend, attack, and even to keep goal. Some very useful players began their careers from similar beginnings.

Football wasn't the only activity at the Pear Street playground. In one corner there was a permanent pitch for playing marbles. It had so much use that it was worn as smooth as a billiard table, and it wasn't only children that used the marble pitch, but also a lot of men who were out of work, filling in their days. Other games also had their seasons. Cricket, with one wicket, if a bat and ball could be had. Tally Ho, a game of chase involving two teams. Conkers, where a horse chestnut was threaded on to a piece of string, each player taking turns to try to break his opponent's chestnut. Certain brands of cigarettes had picture cards and, collected properly, would form sets of fifty, depicting professional footballers, cars, aeroplanes, ships, etc. In the playground, one player would divide his cards and hold them, numbers down, in each hand. The other player would gamble a number of cards on either hand. If he chose the higher number, he won the amount he had gambled, if he chose the lower number, he lost the gambled amount. All very simple.

The girls shared the playground, too. They played 'two-ball'; they skipped, sometimes with a long rope, taking two to keep it turning, while another two or three skipped; hop-scotch; and sometimes with tops and whips. Charlie used to love to hear them chanting their rhymes: 'Pitch, patch, pepper'; 'B-I-N-G-O'; 'two, four, six, eight, Mary at the cottage gate'; 'oranges and lemons': this was while they skipped or played ball.

Charlie said out loud, to himself, 'Aye, they were happy times.'

Most nights, at about eight o'clock, the local policeman, PC Chambers, would walk into the playground. He was a well liked policeman who commanded a lot of respect. He had been a promising professional footballer, but a damaged knee had spoiled that career. He always called the footballing group, his 'raggy arsed rovers'. It was a good description; a lot of their trousers had seen better days. He would usually watch the game for about ten minutes and in that time, the players would give of their best, in the hope of having a few words of encouragement from PC Chambers. Before leaving he would always say, 'Right, lads, let's pick the ball up now; we have to let the babies and the old uns have some peace.' The ball was always picked up immediately.

Then, the playground took on the role of 'the back street university'. Everyone formed into groups; the older lads in the centre were the lecturers, and the younger ones learned the ways of the world, usually with the help of a few smutty stories. For Charlie they were great times.

It was Harry Snowden's tenth birthday. Charlie could remember it like yesterday. Harry lived just a few doors from Charlie and had been bought a proper football for his birthday present. It was a Sunday morning and Harry was in Charlie's mother's kitchen before seven thirty; Charlie was only just out of bed. Harry was there to show off his new ball. It was beautiful, a size five, a proper match-sized ball. They enthused about how all the stitched panels formed a T, how wonderful the new leather smelled, and how smooth and glossy it was to the touch. Harry asked Charlie if he would accompany him to Laurel Close, on the other side of the town. Harry had an uncle there who was caretaker of Laurel Close school. He had promised to inflate the ball for Harry, and lace it up properly. Charlie was delighted to oblige. They carried the ball, still in its tissue paper wrapping, right across the town, taking a good half hour.

Charlie had been warned that Harry's uncle was a bit of a joker, but he never dreamed of how much, until he met him. Harry's aunt answered the door and invited them in. Charlie was amazed at how much alike the uncle and aunt were. They were like matching toby jugs, portly, with round happy faces. They were genuinely pleased to see Harry and Charlie.

'Now then, lads, would you's like a pork sandwich?'

Quick as a flash, Harry answered, 'No thanks, uncle, we've just had our breakfast.'

Charlie thought to himself that Harry was a bit hasty, he could have eaten a pork sandwich.

'It's just as well,' said the uncle, 'We haven't had any pork for months!'

At this the aunt and uncle became creased with laughter. Charlie didn't think it very funny at all. After they had stopped laughing, and dried the tears that were rolling down their cheeks, the uncle said, 'Did you know, King Charles walked and talked an hour after his head was cut off!'

Charlie and Harry were on their guard and waited for the joke. Uncle repeated the sentence, this time altering the emphasis: King Charles walked and talked; an hour after his head was cut off. Again uncle and aunt rolled about with laughter. After the uncle's face had straightened, he looked derogatorily at Charlie and Harry.

'Have you two walked right through town in that state; look at you's, only half a shirt on your back.'

Charlie thought to himself, we are not in what you might call Sunday best, but surely we are not as bad as all that. Then of course was the punch line: 'The other half is on your front.' Once again the aunt and uncle broke into peals of laughter.

'Cor,' thought Charlie, 'I can't take much more of this.'

Uncle took the ball from Harry and commented on its quality. It was clear to see that he was well versed in the art of preparing that type of ball. He placed the inner ball inside the flap and loosely laced it, then inflated it, tied it off and neatly tightened the lace. It was beautifully done. He handed the ball to Harry, and made the only sensible comment that Charlie had heard from him.

'Try to play with it on the grass; if you kick it about the back streets, it will be as thin as a paper bag in a fortnight.'

While the ball was being prepared the aunt had toasted a teacake and thickened it with butter.

'Here you are, lads,' she said, as she handed them half each. 'You can eat that on the road.'

Harry's uncle and aunt, with faces beaming, saw them off.

'Cor, Harry, I'd heard your uncle was a joker, now I know it's right.'

Harry was too wrapped up with his new ball to listen; his face radiated pleasure as he walked toward home. Charlie was pleased to share in his delight.

Walking home they had to pass the church. Just beyond the graveyard wall, there was a triangular area of grass. Harry and Charlie couldn't resist it. They put their jackets down to mark the goal and started a game of 'three goals in'. After a few minutes, three lads of the same age joined them; it was good playing with the new ball. Then the three lads suddenly ran off down the street. He turned to ask Harry what was going on, but then saw Jeremiah Wild. How he'd got there, Charlie couldn't tell, but he was standing with his foot on the new ball, brandishing a four-pronged garden fork. He was dressed in long grey clothes, and had a savage look on his face. He presented a frightening picture to two ten-year-old lads. Charlie and Harry couldn't retrieve the ball; they were forced to stand, and face him. Jeremiah Wild started screaming at them; Charlie thought he was going mad. He was shouting about 'the wrath of God', and 'fire and brimstone'.

Charlie knew what he was going to do with the garden fork, but they could only stand there and take Jeremiah's abuse. He verbally tore into the lads, demanding by what right they had to desecrate the Good Lord's ground by playing ball games on it. He called them scruffy, untidy urchins, who were unfit to breathe the same air as other God-fearing citizens. He would make sure they would not calumniate the Lord's ground again. With a supercilious smirk on his sadistic, swine of a face, he plunged the garden fork right through the new ball. As it was newly inflated, it burst, and a piece was blown out of it.

Jeremiah Wild turned his back on Charlie and Harry and strode towards the church. They picked up the ruined ball and their jackets, and walked back to the street. Harry was heart-broken. In between his sobs and snivels, he cursed and swore at Jeremiah Wild. Charlie didn't know Harry knew so many swear words; he made it very clear what he'd have done to Jeremiah with his garden fork if only he had been a bit bigger. At the top of their street they walked straight into Harry's mother, who evaluated the situation immediately.

'What have you done with your new ball, our Harry?' Her tone was menacing. It was tradition that you fought your own battles, you didn't carry your troubles to your parents. Harry's answer had to be, 'I burst it, Ma.' She grabbed Harry by the scruff of the neck and shook him, as a terrier would shake a rat.

'Come home with me and see what your dad has to say about this.'

Harry had to suffer the humiliation of being dragged down the street bawling his head off, having his 'pants dusted' by his mother. About a week later, when the situation had settled down, Charlie and Harry were walking to school when Harry said in his broad accent, 'Ya naw, Charlie, ah divent think God would a minded us heven a gam o shotty in on his grass.'

'Naw, Harry, ah divent suppose he wad.'

A few weeks later, Charlie became a very reluctant customer at Jeremiah Wild's shop. He had been directed by his mother to run an errand for her. She had run out of blacklead, and it was the day she did the fireplace. Charlie couldn't face Jeremiah, so he made the excuse that there was none in the shop. His mother knew differently; she called him a lazy lump and gave him a clip on the backside. Under duress he returned to the shop. When Jeremiah served him, he gave no indication of recognition; he just gave him the blacklead, handed him his change, and Charlie carried the message home. It was the one and only time Charlie set foot in the shop.

A few months later they had a new teacher at the school, a Miss Raine. She was young and keen, a real interesting person; Charlie enjoyed her lessons. As she was new at the school, she was given the unpopular activities to administer, one of these being physical training sessions. She made these periods interesting by substituting absorbing games for the usual 'physical jerks'. It meant the pupils had their exercise without the tedium. The boys and girls were separated for these sessions. Miss Raine was teaching the girls some simple gymnastics. Of course, at the time, with money so tight, no one had proper gym kit, and Miss Raine had the girls tuck their dresses into their knickers, to allow them freedom of movement. The condition of Jeremiah's daughter's upper legs caught her eye. They were in a dreadful state, the result of years of severe beatings. Miss Raine immediately stopped the session, handed her class to another teacher, and took Ruth to a local doctor. The doctor was appalled at her injuries, but there was nothing he could do in the way of treatment. He accompanied Miss Raine and Ruth back to school, where they reported what they had found to the headmaster. If Ruth had been born a few years later, she would have been taken into care and Jeremiah Wild would have been prosecuted for what he had done to her, but as it was he got off scot free. A furious father came down to the school, bawling about his parental rights. That she had to learn 'the fear of the Lord'. That he had to teach her these things, and that it was a family matter. Unfortunately for Ruth and Miss Raine, there were too many of the 'spare the rod and spoil the child' brigade in the authorities. Jeremiah walked away from the situation and Miss Raine was sacked.

A few years later, when Ruth was only just seventeen years old, she met a young steeplejack, Matt Wilson. He was working on the church when they met, and they were immediately attracted to one another. When Jeremiah Wild heard of the association, he was, as expected, furious. He forbade her to see the young man, and thought he had made sure she wouldn't see him again by keeping her locked in her room, only allowing her out when he himself supervised her.

He awoke one morning to find a ladder at Ruth's window, and her room empty. The couple were too young to be married in England without her parents' consent so ran off to Scotland, where they stayed long enough to satisfy the law in Scotland, and were married.

Matt was a local man, and worked for a firm of steeplejacks. After Ruth and he were married, they came home and set up house in a terrace, close to Matt's work. He was quite a few years older than Ruth, and thought the world of her. He was gentle with her, treasured her, and looked after her better than anyone had done in her whole life. Ruth appreciated all this, and in return she did her best for him. Even with her tender years, she soon learned thrifty housekeeping, and how to make good wholesome meals. After a year, they had a baby girl, and for the first time Ruth enjoyed a normal, natural, happy lifestyle.

When Ruth's baby was four years old, and Matt and Ruth had been together for five years, tragedy struck them. It was a windy day, and Matt's boss decided that the weather was too bad to work on the high factory chimney, which was their project at the time. Instead they would tidy up their builders' yard. There was a lean-to in the yard, with a slate roof; two or three of the slates were loose so Matt decided to put them right. It was only about fourteen feet high, which was virtually on the ground compared to most of their work. Whether this made Matt a little less careful wasn't known. He slipped and fell awkwardly, and broke his neck. The boss sent for Ruth and she cradled Matt in her arms, but within an hour he was dead.

Ruth was devastated, but having to face up to the harsh realities of life cut short her chances of natural grieving. Matt didn't have any other family, so that whole trauma, the distress of the inquest and the funeral fell on Ruth's young shoulders. She would have liked to have kept her home together, mainly for the sake of their daughter, but it just was not possible. She considered all the alternatives. As she was so young, and untrained, she could have only taken menial employment, which certainly wouldn't have paid enough to keep her home together, and the hours would have been long. She would have had to pay someone to look after her daughter. She even lowered herself and applied to the 'parish' for assistance, but because she had a mother and father still alive, nothing was available to her. She was forced to 'eat humble pie', and ask her father if she and her daughter could move back into his home.

Jeremiah Wild made a big thing about pleasing God and doing his Christian duty, such a big sacrifice he was making, but he would take her back. If he had told the truth, he would have admitted that Ruth's mother was in her premature dotage, brought about by his continual unrelenting, cruel, bullying ways. His excuse was always that it 'was the way of the Lord'. His house was no longer kept up to the standard he expected. Having Ruth back would provide an unpaid skivvy for him.

Ruth had been back in her father's house for about six weeks, during which time she cleaned the house, cooked the meals, looked after her daughter and did all the shopping and errands. It was when she came home from one of these errands that all the trouble erupted. She walked in to the all too well known scenario. Her daughter was standing in the corner of the room, sobbing her heart out. Her father was sitting straight-backed in the wooden chair, the three foot long cane by his side, ranting about the child having 'to learn the ways of the Lord'. Her mother hovered in the background, afraid to comfort the child. Ruth walked over to her daughter, lifted her dress, and examined the evidence of the thrashing she had received from Jeremiah.

All the bottled-up emotions boiled to the surface. Her suppressed grief over Matt's death. Her heartache, and all the unanswered questions as to why it had had to happen to him, to cause her so much anguish. The beating of her daughter was the last straw. There was no way she could accept that her daughter would go through her childhood in the same manner as she had had to endure, living in constant fear, her character smothered, her personality unable to develop, hardly daring to breathe, in case it was out of place. Ruth walked to the bread board, picked up the gully, and plunged it into Jeremiah's heart. He died in seconds.

After three months in jail, Ruth appeared before a judge and jury, at the Assize Court. The prosecuting counsel was by far the most dominating; in fact Ruth's counsel was hopeless. Perhaps he felt he didn't have a chance with the case, or perhaps he was too young and inexperienced, but he didn't bring any of the mitigating circumstances to the attention of the jury. Between the prosecuting counsel and the newspapers, Ruth came over as the wicked, cruel daughter, who had repaid her father, who had taken her in when she was in poor circumstances, by stabbing him through the heart. They portrayed Jeremiah as a good church-going man, whose only sin had been to chastise Ruth's daughter. The jury were not shown the brutal, sadistic, side of the man, whose real name turned out to be Edward. Jeremiah was a name he had cooked up to impress the church. The judge, in his final instructions to the jury, could only say that Edward had died because he had chastised his grand-daughter.

It only took the jury one hour to find Ruth guilty of murdering her father. The judge passed the only sentence he could. Ruth was to be hanged. Her counsel launched an appeal, but it was a very weak effort and was turned down; the sentence was to stand. The date was set for the execution: it was to be a month later. Again the newspapers had a field day; not one of them had a decent word for her.

A week later, the town began to realise what an horrendous thing was to be done to Ruth. People talked amongst themselves, and opinion moved Ruth's way. People knew Edward Wild was not the saint that he had been painted at the trial, nor was she the villain, as she had been portrayed. She most certainly didn't deserve to die for what she had done.

A retired vicar, who had worked for the local church some years earlier, came back to the town and organised a petition to be taken to London, to the Home Secretary. It was a plea to have Ruth's life spared. He obviously knew of Edward Wild's ways. The petition was worded as a letter to the Home Secretary, and stated that the trial of Ruth Wilson had not brought out the real truth of what had happened, that the death sentence passed upon her was too harsh and that the undersigned were asking him to review her case. There was a full writing pad available for anyone who wanted to sign and a small wooden box beside the petition to collect money from anyone who wished to contribute to the expenses of taking the petition to London. It was kept unlocked, at the entrance to the Council Offices. There was a steady flow of people keen to sign and leave money for the expenses. The door was ever open, Barnforth wasn't the most honest of places, yet the money was never touched.

41

On the Sunday afternoon just after the petition had been launched, Charlie had a surprise visitor. It was Harry Snowden. Harry had married and moved to East Bullfield, a small colliery village about four miles out of town. Charlie's mother made them a cup of tea and they sat talking as they drank it. Harry came straight to the point of the visit. In his broad dialect he said, 'Ah heared they had a petition up to try and stop them from hingen Ruth.'

'And have you come to sign?' said Charlie.

'Sign, look at here,' said Harry, as he held up a sheaf of papers. 'Ah've been roond every hoose in East Bullfield, an they've all signed.' He patted his pocket and carried on, 'An' they've given a pocketful of money, to pur in the box, an a'v walked all the way here, an a'll walk all the way home, so as ah can put me bus fare in the box.'

Charlie offered to walk into town with him, to deliver the signatures and money. Inevitably, as they walked down, the conversation centred on Ruth's trial.

'Hinged, Charlie, she should niver be hinged, the' must be hundreds who would have liked to have done the rotten ahd swine in, me included for what he did ta my new ball that day. Ah'v often thowt what ah'd hev liked ta dee we that garden fork. So she shouldn't be hinged, in fact she should be given a medal as big as Ganny Stokes' frying pan.'

Ganny Stokes had a husband and five sons, all doing heavy manual work. She was purported to have a colliery-made frying pan, as big as a dustbin lid.

With just a few days to go before the execution date, the names on the petition were counted. There were thousands of signatures and, most surprisingly, £385, a fortune in those days.

The vicar had connections in London, and was to take the petition, accompanied by his wife. Arrangements had been made for him to have a personal meeting with the Home Secretary's personal private secretary. The only money they took from the collecting box was their train fare to London; the rest was put in trust for Ruth's daughter.

Circumstances were again not to go Ruth's way. The vicar and his wife were decoyed into an alley by a young woman who asked them to help her with a sick friend. Whilst in the alley they were set upon by a gang, and were beaten, robbed, and left unconscious. Because the couple were in hospital, badly concussed, they were unable to keep the arranged meeting. The petition was never delivered.

The sentence was carried out. Ruth was hanged for the murder of her father. The town seemed to take on the mantle of guilt, and it was weeks before the cloud of gloom began to clear. Ruth's mother was in no position, health-wise, to take on the responsibility of raising her grand-daughter. The one good thing that came out of the whole sad affair was that because of all the publicity given to the trial by the newspapers, couples were clamouring to adopt the child. The authorities eventually chose a wealthy landowner to be her new family. They kept her Christian name, Sally, but her new surname was Ferguson. They didn't attempt to hide Sally's beginnings from her. When she was old enough to understand, she was told the whole story of her real father and mother. She now lived well away from the area.

As Sally grew up she became a regular visitor to the town. Always, on the anniversary of her mother's death, she would be in the town to place flowers on her mother's grave. The news of her arrival always spread quickly, as her poise, composure, dress culture and sophistication stood out head and shoulders above most in the town. Charlie saw her on two or three of these occasions, and knew Ruth would have been proud of her. She tried regularly to obtain permission to have her mother's body moved to be buried in the same grave as her father, and her attempts always made the newspapers. The authorities would have none of it. Ruth had to lie in an unconsecrated graveyard within the confines of the prison.

Charlie took a lingering look at the garish shop, and felt a shiver run down his spine, not from the slight chill in the air.

CHAPTER 8

In a cul-de-sac just past Jeremiah Wild's shop, years ago, two or three market traders used to set up their stalls on a Saturday afternoon. They were popular with the town people, but were in constant conflict with the shopkeepers, because unlike them they didn't pay local taxes. The shopkeepers argued that the traders had an unfair advantage. For the same reason they were discouraged by the local authority.

There were two stalls that Charlie distinctly remembered. One of them was a middle-aged woman who ran a fruit and vegetable stall. The other was an older man, with a pronounced limp, who sold second hand books, magazines and comics. Charlie had been a very ashamed customer at the book stall. If he took a friend with him, each of them would go to a different end of the stall. While the man attended to one of them, the other would help himself to a handful of second-hand magazines from the pile. The old man was so slow to turn around, there wasn't a chance of being caught. Remembering what he had done filled Charlie with remorse. He consoled himself by thinking that if the old man had still been alive, he might have pushed a five pound note into his hand, the one he was going to spend in the supermarket. There again, Charlie didn't believe in charity. Besides, he had put a pound in the collecting plate at Fred's funeral, something else he didn't believe in. He took solace in the thought of his pound on the collecting plate, and that relieved his feeling of guilt.

It was the thought of the woman who ran the fruit and vegetable stall that stirred the funniest memories for Charlie.

Charlie, Fred and another two friends were sitting in the White Swan. They had all had a few pints of beer and had played dominoes for a couple of hours and were preparing for home. They were playing a simple last game with the dominoes. Each put threepence in the kitty, then they turned the dominoes face down on the board, shuffled them and each of them in turn picked up one domino and placed it in the small wooden box. The one who picked up the last 'double' won the kitty. It was an interesting way of having the dominoes put away. It was when this game was finished, and they were talking and finishing their drinks, that Fred made his shock announcement: 'I think I've fallen in love today.'

It was as if the Queen had told the nation in her Christmas day broadcast that she was giving up the kingdom and taking up marbles! Charlie spluttered in his beer, the other two burst out laughing, and one of them said, 'Come on, Fred, tell us who the lucky lady is.'

'I'll make no bones about it. It's the woman with the fruit and veg stall, down at the Saturday market.'

Still laughing, the same chap said, 'But Fred man, she's as ugly as a rhubarb root.'

'I admit she's no bathing beauty, but to me she's lovely. If you'll all stop giggling like schoolgirls I'll tell you's about it. You all know what sort of a time ah've been having of it lately. Ah've drawn a bad cable, at the pit. Ah'm in the Lower Busty seam; it was always a good'un, but we've hit a fault, we're struggling to make the mini. I'm not joking when Ah say, Ah haven't heard a pleasant word for months. The pit manager's twisting his face, so is the deputy and the overman and, of course, the rest of the men. The missus is not suited, and Ah can understand that; in fact if it wasn't for the free house, we wouldn't be able to eat properly, so she's nag, nag, nagging on at me all the time. An' there's the two lads. Ah can only give them coppers for their pocket money, so they're moaning on at me all the time into the bargain. Ah was just about at the end of me tether with them. Ah got in the house about three o'clock Saturday afternoon, an' the Missus was straight on at me. The taties at the fruit and veg stall were tuppence a stone cheaper than the shop, she needed a stone, and if Ah thought she was carrying them, Ah could think again.

'Well, if you's remember, it drizzled on raining all Saturday afternoon, so Ah was wet, to add to all the other miseries and discomforts. To keep the peace, Ah made me way down to the stall. Do you know, that stall-holder woman, she smiled at me, just at me, mind you, and such a lovely smile, and she pinched my cheek an' said, "Come on, me old darlin', lets see ya cheered up a bit, life's not as bad as all that." Do

45

you's know, Ah floated home with that stone of taties. That woman she melted my heart, an' Ah'll tell ya, if she had snapped her fingers at me, Ah'd have followed her to the ends of the world. Aye, an' stepped off.'

Charlie and the other two had laughed at Fred, but it was to cover emotions they couldn't quite grasp. It still amused Charlie to think of the incident; it was another link in the chain of good memories of his friend Fred.

CHAPTER 9

Over the next few weeks, Charlie's sister gradually worsened. All the neighbours were concerned about her illness, and there was always a steady stream of visitors. Charlie listened carefully to the different diagnoses put forward by the more knowledgeable ladies: 'She's outgrown her strength, and needs building up,' was one opinion; 'It's a wasting disease,' was another thought. Looking back, Charlie now knew it had in fact been leukaemia. There was nothing Doctor Gordon could do, other than administer pain killers and recommend good nursing to keep her comfortable.

At first it was quite easy for Charlie's mother to do the necessary nursing, as Hannah was able to help herself in many ways. As the disease progressed, she weakened. The burden would soon have become unsustainable but luckily they had very good neighbours, who looked on the tragedy of Hannah's illness to be equally their responsibility. They soon organised themselves so that there was always someone available, night or day.

Before leaving for his shift at the foundry, Charlie got into the habit of visiting his sister's sickroom, where he would drink his mug of tea, have a few words with Hannah, and listen to the chat of whichever neighbour was assisting with the nursing. They all put on a cheerful attitude, in an effort to keep Hannah's spirits up, and they rarely came empty-handed, bringing perhaps something like a couple of fresh eggs, or a tasty bite from their baking days. Their kindness was really touching, and much appreciated by both Hannah and her mother.

Charlie didn't realise how much their help meant until one evening Doctor Gordon called and offered Hannah a bed in a hospice run by a charity. It would have been free. He left them to think it over, and called back the following day.

Charlie's mother thanked him with the words, 'Doctor, Hannah and

I have discussed your kind offer. Let's face it, Hannah knows, the same as you and I know, what the outcome of this illness is. If it's all the same with you, she'd rather spend what time she has left with her family, friends, and neighbours. I know you mean well with the offer of a place in the hospice, and I know you're doing this to take some of the weight from my shoulders, but the neighbours are very good and are helping me with the nursing, day and night. If you will continue tending her when necessary, and keep prescribing the medicine, we'll manage.'

The doctor replied, 'You know I'll do all I can for Hannah. May I add, you and your neighbours are keeping her every bit as comfortable as the hospice could, and a deal happier. Good evening to you, I'll look in tomorrow.'

The next morning, Charlie tapped on his sister's bedroom door, his mug of tea in his hand; it was about seven a.m. Young Billy Raine's wife, from the opposite side of the street, was in attendance. She was sitting Hannah up, prior to tempting her with milky porridge and tea, which was Hannah's favourite breakfast. Irene Raine never stopped talking, and was a bit of a comedienne, Charlie thought she would have been a good turn in a variety sow. Poor Billy, her husband, was the butt of all her stories. She ran him down at every opportunity, with every derogatory phrase she could lay her tongue to. Everyone knew it was all just a sham; she thought the world of him really. It would have been 'God help' anyone else who made a critical remark about him.

'Do you think we should let him in, Hannah?' she said and, answering her own question, went on, 'I suppose if he keeps his nose clean, he can have five minutes,'

Irene didn't seem to stop talking, even to draw breath; both Hannah and Charlie enjoyed listening to her. Charlie stood by the bed sipping his tea.

'I can come in every morning at this time, cause Billy has had to go on permanent fore shift. I'll tell you how it came about. You know our Joseph has troubles with his teeth.' Joseph was her ten-year-old son. 'Well, Doctor Gordon advised us to take him to a dentist at Longtown Acres. Old Henry Whats-his-name, the dentist down the High Street, he's too old, not up to modern thinking. He was going to pull them all out, wait a year or two, and make him a set of false ones, they're his second teeth, you know. I ask you, to be so young and saddled with false teeth. We took the doctor's advice and took him to see the young dentist at Longtown Acres. He explained to us how Joseph has a very small jaw, not enough room for all his teeth. He showed us the teeth he would remove, and he'd make a sort of splint to straighten the others up. It'd be an expensive job, twenty-four pounds he said it would cost, and we couldn't have afforded it, but his granny had an insurance policy up, so she's paying most of it, and by, we're grateful.

'Last Wednesday our Billy, the great useless tatie, he hasn't as many brains as a whelk, took Joseph for his appointment at the dentist to have the selected teeth removed. His appointment was for two o'clock in the afternoon. It was seven o'clock when they landed home. It's only a half-hour journey, they should have been home by three thirty. I didn't know what had happened; I was frantic with worry.

'What happened was, when they came out of the dentist's, they'd gone to Swainston's shop, that big one that sells toys, china, cycles, prams, and the like. Billy had put every penny he had in his pocket off a bike for our Joseph's Christmas, and joined the Christmas club, to pay off the remainder. Mind, it's a lovely bike, if I have to say so myself. A Rudge Whitworth, with a three speed gear, and dynamo and battery lights. Its total price is £4 9s. 6d. It means he has to pay six shillings a fortnight into the club.

'When they came out of the shop and caught the bus for home, as soon as the bus started to move, Joseph felt sick. It was because of the anaesthetic gas he'd been given at the dentist's. They had to make a hurried exit from the bus, and of course it went off without them. They waited half an hour for the next bus, but the conductor had taken their return tickets. With Billy having spent all his money, this conductor put them off the bus. They had to walk home, with Joseph only groggy from having his teeth out.

'Well, I heard what had happened, what that brainless Billy had done, not just the worry he'd caused me, but it's not fair on our Beth.' Beth was their nine-year-old daughter. 'Well, you can't spend all that money on a bike for one of them, and leave the other out, can you?' She didn't wait for an answer. 'I dragged him back to the same shop on Friday, and made him put his name down for a dolly and pram for Beth; it's another five shillings a fortnight. I only give him seven an' six back out of his pay for his pocket, and he has the dog to feed out of that, and he likes the odd glass of beer.

'As I say, he's had to go on permanent fore shift, so he can have his afternoons free. The thick-headed mindless lump has taken on a job for Alex Brass, the farmer; he's cutting and laying a big rough hawthorn hedge for him. The senseless ha'p'orth, he's working like a brainless cuddy, and Alex Brass is only paying him three shillings a chain.'

With her hand half shielding her face, she gave Hannah a big wink, and, in a stage whisper, with a big grin on her face, said, 'Mind, it keeps him out of mischief.'

Charlie had to say quick good-byes and run down the street or he would have been late for work. 'She can sure tell a story,' Charlie thought to himself.

CHAPTER 10

His name being called from the other side of the street brought Charlie abruptly out of his day-dreams. It was Andrew Brown who had the newsagent's shop. Charlie had always liked a couple of shillings on the horses. All his adult life, he had been a customer at the newsagent's and had a newspaper delivered daily, mainly for weighing up the racing form. He always called at the shop every Saturday afternoon to settle his bill. Andrew was about the same age as Charlie and was officially retired; the shop was run by his adopted daughter Eve, but he was still a capable man and helped out where he could. Charlie answered his call, and thanked heaven they were on opposite sides of the street, for Andrew liked a 'chin wag' and would have kept Charlie talking for an hour or more. On many Saturday afternoons Charlie would hide round the corner of the shop, hoping to see Andrew talking to another customer. He would then take the chance to nip in, pay his bill to Eve, and beat a quick retreat. Andrew had been a hard working man for the whole of his life; it was only since his retirement that he would pass the time with a chat. In his younger days you were fortunate if you heard two words from him.

When he was about eight years old, he took a dislike to school. He liked nothing better than spending his days truanting on any of a dozen farms, all within walking distance of the school. The farmers were as much to blame as anyone for his truancy. They encouraged him by giving him little jobs to do, usually paying him a few coppers and his dinner each day. His parents and the headmaster tried everything to keep him in school. They thrashed him, to no avail. They threatened him with Borstal, to no avail. They talked to him for hours to try and impress on him the importance of a good education, all to no avail. Even if his mother led him to school by the hand, the first open door was all Andrew needed to be off. He would be on one of the farms before his mother was home. He was a likeable lad, not cheeky in any way. He took his thrashings like a man, and he stood quietly and listened to advice. He just couldn't stand being confined; he would rather job about in the open, on a farm, than go to school.

Andrew's last day at school was a memorable one and was talked about for years. He would have been about eleven years old, and was truanting as usual, when the school board man came on to the farm where he was working, and collared him. Andrew was put into the kid-catcher's car and driven to school. It was morning playtime when they arrived and, with a triumphant smirk on his face, the kid-catcher marched Andrew across the school yard. Everybody stopped what they were doing and watched in silence as Andrew was frog-marched into school. Halfway over the yard, Andrew caught sight of the open side gate; with a quick wriggle he left the kid-catcher holding his empty jacket and made a bolt for it. Unfortunately for Andrew, one of the teachers was two paces too fast for him. He barred his route to freedom. Andrew panicked, and raced about the yard like a headless chicken.

All the other kids in the yard screamed with delight at the situation, half of them trying to keep him in school, the other half trying to help him escape; it was utter chaos. Eventually one of the lads gripped the five foot high fence and made a type of stile with his body. Andrew jumped on the lad's back, and was over. Still in blind panic, he ran across the road.

At the time there were only about a dozen private cars in the town. By sheer bad luck, two of them were passing the school at the same time. To miss Andrew one of them braked hard and swerved into the path of the other. They became locked together by their bumpers. Still locked together they careered across the road, straight into the truant catcher's car that was parked by the school gate. One of the cars was a very old type, with the petrol tank under the bonnet. It ruptured with the force of the collision, spilling petrol under the three cars. The hot engine ignited the fuel.

Andrew's last sight of the scene was the owners looking on while their cars went up in flames. Andrew didn't dare go home. He hid in woodland until it was darkening, then made his way to the river. He walked most of the night, following the river upstream. Although he only travelled about ten miles, the countryside was entirely different to what he was used to. It was hill and moorland. Farms were few and far between. Even so, he still found the odd day's work, for which, as usual, he was paid his few coppers and given an occasional meal. Having to sleep out and live rough, he soon became dirty, and his clothes ragged. Farmers no longer wanted him on their property. He was soon having to steal food, just to survive.

After about three weeks, his health gave out. A farmer found him one morning lying in a hemmel in a remote part of his farm. He was desperately ill. The farmer put him into his horse-drawn cart and took him back to the farmhouse. His wife had nursing experience and soon weighed up how ill Andrew was. She sent for a doctor, put him in a clean warm bed and bathed him.

When the doctor arrived, he found Andrew with a raging fever and great difficulty with his breathing. He prescribed treatment. As Andrew was unknown in the district, with him being so ill, the doctor informed the police. By the middle of the afternoon, Andrew had double pneumonia and his mother had arrived at the farmhouse. It hadn't been difficult for the police to discover who Andrew was. For a week, Andrew lay at death's door. He had to stay at the farmhouse, as he was too ill to be moved. The farmer's wife was very good, and allowed his mother to stay with him in the farmhouse. Between them they nursed him.

It was five weeks before the doctor would allow Andrew to return home and several months before he regained all of his strength. He was never made to return to school. His mother didn't make him and the education officials never sent for him. It left Andrew free to do what he liked best, and that was working on the local farms. He was in steady demand by the farmers, for even though he was so young, he had spent so much time about the farms that he had the knowledge and the ability to do many of the tasks that could have been expected of a much older person.

When Andrew reached employable age, he obtained a job with James Gibson, a well-to-do farmer and cattle dealer. His farm was near the village of High Tramley, about ten miles from Andrew's home. It was impractical for him to travel, so he was given an attic room in the farmhouse to sleep in and his meals, as part of his wages. James Gibson's family consisted of wife, two sons, and a daughter, all of them vain and useless. Andrew's employer was not as good as he thought he was, either. He was unable to give proper instructions to his men, the result being that things often went seriously wrong. Andrew couldn't count how many times he had heard Mr Gibson ranting about his 'damned useless men'. Consequently his employees didn't stay very long with him.

Andrew, for all he was only fourteen years old, knew what was needed. He had, of course, been around a variety of farms for several years. He quietly got on with the task of pulling the farm together and was very soon the king pin in the farming side of Mr Gibson's business. The other men looked to him for guidance.

If Mr Gibson could have seen it, he had an absolute gem-stone in Andrew, but like the rest of his family, he was too tied up in his own importance. His two sons and daughter did nothing in the work line; their only interests were social events and the local hunt. They each had their own hunter stabled at the farm. Most days they appeared around mid-day, strutting around the stable area dressed in their expensive riding apparel. They angered Andrew, especially when they would call men from urgent tasks to feed and clean their horses for them. The elder boy markedly enraged Andrew, for he was arrogant and disdainful. He always carried an ivory handled riding crop which he continually beat on his riding boot. The habit really touched a sore spot with Andrew.

Even though Andrew lived in the house with the family, he was never allowed in the parlour or the dining room. He was confined to his attic bedroom for which he had to use the back stairs, and the kitchen where he was allowed to eat his meals. The only friend he had in the house was Lena, the housekeeper. She was a middle aged, genial woman, without a 'picking' on her, and far over worked. The family expected far too much of her. Every night, after his work, Andrew would help her in any way he could. He would gladly lift anything that was too heavy for her, and carry the four buckets of coal that were used in the parlour each evening. She, in turn, would see that Andrew had the best food she could manage. Unfortunately Lena finished work at six o'clock each evening and left to go home, leaving Andrew with long lonely evenings.

It wasn't so bad in the summer-time, when he could fill in his time doing odd jobs about the farm or taking walks around the village, but the dark winter nights were hard for him. It was always cold, the only heating being the kitchen stove which had to be out before six o'clock and relaid, so Lena just had to put a match to it first thing in the mornings.

Because of his lack of education, he was unable to read to pass the time. He tried knitting and embroidery, but it was so cold, it was impossible to concentrate. All that was left for him was to retire to his bed very early on these nights.

This routine carried on for about three years, Andrew gradually pulling the farm into shape, his talents and hard work unrecognised and unappreciated. He could go for weeks on end and never hear a pleasant word.

Then suddenly it all changed, Eunice, the daughter, who was about four years older than Andrew, took a shine to him. It was embarrassing, as he was far too young for the sort of relationship she had in mind. Andrew was scared. If her family found out, their reactions didn't bear thinking about. She wouldn't be discouraged but pursued him relentlessly. Eventually, as was bound to happen, Mr Gibson found them kissing in the stable. Andrew was given five minutes to pack his belongings and leave the farm.

Andrew was only unemployed for two hours. Lord John, a neighbouring landowner, when he heard what had happened, sought Andrew out, offering him a job and a small house to go with it. Lord John was not really his name. He was John Lord, but he was a real gentleman, so the title fitted him. All the locals called him Lord John, even to his face; sometimes he even had mail delivered with the title. He owned an estate of five farms, four of them let to tenant farmers. The Home Farm, he farmed himself. There was no love lost between him and Mr Gibson; in fact they couldn't stand each other. Employing Andrew was an one-upmanship thing, a sort of feather in his cap for Lord John.

The working environment was much better, as Lord John, himself a hard working man, could appreciate the efforts that Andrew put into his work.

Home life was now very different for him, but cooking for himself the hardest part to become used to as he was very short of the domestic niceties and all he had to cook on was a two-burner paraffin oil stove, given to him by his mother. Having to set up home so unexpectedly meant he had to depend on bits and pieces, borrowed or given. After about a couple of weeks he had the basics: a rickety bed, two wobbly kitchen chairs, a table that needed to be spragged under one leg, a length of coco-matting for the floor, and the stove. The luxury which he appreciated most was that he now had a fireside; he could take comfort sitting by a wood fire for an hour before going to bed.

Sacking Andrew didn't solve Mr Gibson's problem. Eunice was a very strong willed girl, used to getting her own way. She had set her cap for Andrew and wouldn't be dissuaded. She was soon a regular visitor to Andrew's house. Using her considerable guile she soon had Andrew talking marriage. He was by no means ready for such a step, but was no match for Eunice's determination. She settled all resistance from home by announcing that she was pregnant, which wasn't true. She then made plans with Andrew, and they went ahead with a civil marriage ceremony at the Town Hall.

Although there was no great love between them, there was genuine affection, and she did her best for him. She didn't have many housekeeping skills, but she was an intelligent girl and soon learned the basics. She had ambitions for Andrew, aiming for them eventually to take a farm and farm it themselves.

Had they been left alone, they would probably have made a good marriage, but it wasn't to be. Eunice did become pregnant and at about seven months into the pregnancy she was having some problems. They called on a young doctor who had just recently set up practice in the area. The doctor was a forthright young man and, after examining her, said, 'Eunice, you are not the ideal child-bearing build, you have very narrow hips, and with this being your first child I strongly recommend that you allow me to deliver the baby at the cottage hospital. I know that a lot of people will pooh-pooh the idea of having the baby at the hospital, as they all think all babies should be born at home. In this case I would be much happier delivering your baby at the hospital, where more facilities are available. It will be a bit expensive for you, I would think the charge will be something like twelve to fifteen pounds, but they won't press for payment. If you pay a little as and when you can afford it, they'll be quite happy to accept that.'

Eunice and Andrew accepted his recommendation, and were to call nearer the time to make the final arrangements. They thanked him, and left.

A fortnight later Mr and Mrs Gibson arrived at their house, to make their peace, as they put it. Before the evening was out they had talked Andrew over into letting Eunice go back to the farm with them, where she could be better looked after until after the baby was born. Andrew could go over every evening to see her. Andrew wasn't happy with the idea, but Eunice wanted to go, and as usual, she had her way.

On Andrew's second visit to the farm old Dr Robbs was in attendance. He had examined Eunice and was standing in the parlour, a glass of whisky in his hand, chatting to Mr and Mrs Gibson and the two brothers.

Mr Gibson greeted Andrew, 'Come in, young fellow, meet Charles, er, Dr Robbs to you. He's had a look at our Eunice, and has agreed to deliver the baby for her.'

Andrew answered, 'But we have been to the new doctor in the village; he said it would be better, because of Eunice's shape, if he delivered her baby in the hospital.'

'Never heard such damned nonsense, cheeky young pup, how dare he say my daughter is a bad shape, he'll get a piece of my mind when I see him, Charles has delivered hundreds of babies, all at home, including my three, all without any trouble. Charles has looked at Eunice and everything is perfectly straightforward, so let's not hear any more of this drivel.'

Andrew, being so young and overawed by the Gibson family, had to agree to their plans, even though he was sure that she would have been in much better hands with the new young doctor.

The time came for Eunice to have the baby. As predicted by the young doctor, she had a terrible time, twenty-four hours in labour. The stress was too much for the baby boy and he died in the process. If Eunice had not been so strong, fit and healthy she too could have died.

Andrew felt the loss of the baby boy very deeply, but the situation he was in made it very difficult to show his emotions. Eunice was slow to recover from the trauma of the extremely difficult childbirth, and it was several weeks before she regained much of her strength. Although it was hard for Andrew, he called every evening to see her and could feel the animosity from her family every time he passed through the door. Each evening there were excuses as to why she couldn't return to her home. In his heart he could feel it was all over between Eunice and him.

The latest reason was that the whole Gibson family were invited to the wedding of Mrs Gibson's niece in Hampshire. They'd be away for a long week-end, and they made it very clear that Andrew wasn't invited. He thought no more of the wedding until the middle of the week, when he knew the family would be home. He was steeling himself for the ordeal of his usual visit, when a chauffeur-driven car arrived at his house. It was the father of the bride. He introduced himself to Andrew, and asked if he might come in. He was a real gentleman in his early sixties, well dressed and beautifully spoken.

'I take it you are our Eunice's husband?'

'Yes,' Andrew answered.

'I've driven all the way from Hampshire to apologise personally to you, damned bad form to invite your wife to the wedding and not yourself, but we had no idea that Eunice was married; my wife's sister didn't have the grace to inform us. I really mean it when I say how bad I feel.'

Andrew was beginning to feel uncomfortable at the gentleman's apologies and, to put him at his ease, he told him how unpopular his marriage to Eunice was. The gentleman sat quietly for a while, then told Andrew he was staying the night at the Railway Hotel and asked Andrew to join him for dinner. Andrew refused at first, but the gentleman was insistent.

Andrew dressed himself as best he could and accompanied Robert, as he had been told to address him, in the chauffeur-driven car to the Railway Hotel. He felt uncomfortable, as his dress was far from suitable, but Robert seemed to accept him as he was, so he soon settled down to the meal. It was a most enjoyable evening. Robert was easy to talk with, and Andrew had the whole story of his relationship with Eunice drawn from him. Robert then told him of his life.

'I'm retired now. I've worked in India for this last twenty-five years. I've been managing a tea plantation for one of the big companies. We knew I was to retire this year, so my wife and daughter returned last year to prepare for the wedding, and to have our house made ready for our retirement.'

Robert brought out cigars and offered one to Andrew which he refused. He puffed slowly and carried on with the conversation.

'Eunice isn't a bad girl, and I think, given the chance, will probably make a good wife, but to have any sort of a chance you must get her away from that damned lazy, ignorant, opinionated household. As you will have gathered, personally I cannot stand them. I still have good connections with my old firm. I could secure you a position with them and, if I'm any judge of character, in a very short time you will be managing an Indian tea plantation, just as I was, with a large house full of servants, and the life style of an earl, to boot.'

Robert relit his cigar and told Andrew he intended to call on the Gibson family the following day, to remonstrate with them for putting him in this embarrassing situation. 'It's just not on, don't you know!' was his final word on the subject.

Andrew was driven home by the chauffeur. He sat for an hour by the empty grate and pondered over the opportunity that he had been given. He contemplated his lack of education, and also knew in the back of his mind that even if he could persuade Eunice to go with him to India, the family would never allow it, and he would never be able to talk them round. He would stay where he was, and continue to work for Lord John.

The following evening he made his call on Eunice, and was somewhat taken aback to find he was actually welcomed by Mr and Mrs Gibson. He raked his mind for the reason, and made the mistake of thinking that Robert's visit to the Gibsons had somehow shown himself in a better light.

How wrong he was. It was Mr Gibson's last effort to part Eunice and him forever. Before the evening was out Andrew was invited to accompany Eunice and the rest of the family to the Hunt Ball, which was to be held a week later. Mr Gibson wouldn't take a refusal, or listen to any of Andrew's excuses, his trump card being that he didn't have the appropriate apparel to wear for such an occasion.

'Don't worry about it, Andrew, we have an evening suit here. It won't quite fit you, but Mrs Gibson and Lena will do a few alterations on it, it'll do you fine.'

Andrew didn't have any option other than to agree to go with them. The dread of the event built up in him over the week, and it worsened when he came to dress in the evening suit provided by Mr Gibson.

Lena said it would fit Phyllagalloo, whoever he was; he must have been an awfully big man. The suit had been cut down in an effort to make it fit, but it was so big to start with, it wasn't possible to make any sort of job of it. Andrew didn't have much dress sense, but he knew that he was a mess.

It was the longest, most distressing, evening he had ever spent in his life. From the moment they passed through the doors into the ballroom Andrew was abandoned by the Gibsons and left to his own devices. All the patrons of the ball were a close clique, and strangers, especially his type, were not welcomed into it. Everywhere he turned he was ostracized; groups closed up and backs were turned on him. He lost count of how many times he saw backs slapped, and how many times he heard exaggerated laughs at weak quips as acquaintances met.

There was a big turnout for the event, and most of those in attendance were loud-mouthed. Andrew couldn't help overhearing the conversations. Without exception the topic was hunting and horses. The phrases were so repetitive: 'good bold jumper'; 'gallop all day, and not show one drop of sweat'; 'straightforward mover'; 'a little too fine-legged for my liking'; 'wonderful temperament'; 'a bit prone to colic'; 'good mane, and well feathered'.

Andrew was so out of place, so overwhelmed, in so much of a predicament, he didn't know where to put himself for ease. The ballroom was just one large hall; the only real escape for him would have been to have left the whole proceedings, and as there was only one exit he would have had to walk through the main door. For some reason that he could not fathom, he wasn't prepared to do that. He would see the evening through, whatever mental strain it took.

Eunice was in her element; she was a good dancer and never short of a partner. She was so full of energy, she took part in every dance, often throwing her head back and laughing with her partner. Andrew thought he should have had some sort of jealous feelings toward her, but he didn't; it was all over between them 'bar the shouting' as his mother would have said.

Andrew eased himself slowly through the crowd to some seats in the corner. When he sat down his clothes didn't feel quite so bad, not quite the mess he was when standing up. He had only been seated for about five minutes when a young girl of about his own age came over and sat with him. They were soon chatting together. She was good company, very easy to talk to and feeling as much out of place as Andrew, but considerably better dressed. A kindred spirit, so to speak. He knew a little of her history, as he had overheard two young men discussing her earlier. They had 'silver spoon' accents you could have cut with a knife. In different circumstances he would have laughed at them.

From the conversation he learned that her name was Ellen, and that she was a big disappointment to her grandfather. The one who had told the story had said, 'I was at the meet, don't you know, when she was "blooded". It was in that small copse halfway down Three Sisters Lane. We cornered a cub; mind, it was a bit gruesome, the hounds tore the damned thing limb from limb, ha-ha. Her grandfather "blooded" her with it, and, don't you know, the soft ha'porth ran screaming from the wood. Left her grandfather speechless with rage, and with the two horses to boot! I don't think she's been to another meet. Great disappointment, great disappointment.'

The diversion of her company eased his miseries for a while. They had laughed together when she offered to teach him to waltz, insisting she meant it, but she wasn't allowed the chance. An old crone who was bedecked with jewellery and over made-up came through the crowd like an ocean liner in full steam, and whisked Ellen away without so much as an excuse me to Andrew. He was alone again to endure the miseries he was being put through.

The evening did come to an end. Andrew was never more relieved to return to the Gibsons' home, very conscious of the self-satisfied smirks on their faces. He couldn't change into his own clothes quickly enough to allow him to get out into the darkness and walk back to his own house. On the journey the tears welled up in his eyes, with anger at what he had been put through. He had known from the minute he had walked into the ballroom what the Gibsons were about. The whole exercise had been to show him the difference in their classes. They had wasted their time and efforts, Andrew wanted out every bit as much as they did, but he had no idea how their marriage could be undone.

After the fiasco of the Hunt Ball, Andrew's visits to Eunice became few and far between. Mr Gibson was still not finished with his ploy. He insisted that Andrew accompany them to the County Agricultural Show, and wouldn't take no for an answer. They arrived at the Show and were admitted to the Members' marquee; there was also part of the grandstand for the use of members only. Andrew's heart sank when he saw that the members were the same clique as had attended the Hunt Ball. There was the same back-slapping, and the same exaggerated laughs from the same weak quips. Only this time he wasn't the same type of prisoner as he had been at the Hunt Ball. The showground was big, and there were other events besides the horse jumping.

Andrew walked from the marquee and met a lot of ordinary farmers, their wives, their families and their workpeople. They were people he had met whilst truanting from school; he had worked with them in the past and had had meals with them; they were all pleased to see him. He had a wonderful time, looking at the prize cattle, sheep, pigs and poultry. With the farmers he looked round the trade stands. They examined the new innovations, which were designed to assist the farmers in their everyday work. Some he approved of, others he didn't. The farmers he had teamed up with were well known to many of the trade representatives, and they were invited into their small marquees and plied with tea, sandwiches, or perhaps a half pint of beer.

Andrew had a most enjoyable afternoon. He was encouraged to enter the sheaf-casting competition, coming second and winning twenty-five shillings. He thought he could probably have won the competition had he had the right pitch-fork. There were two available, one of them eight or nine inches shorter than the other. Andrew favoured the shorter one, but one great hulk of a man, with more strength than brains, broke its shaft and ruined Andrew's chance of winning. The prize for winning would have been two pounds, but twenty-five shillings wasn't too bad for his efforts.

Everything considered, Andrew had had a good day. Having to travel home with the Gibsons dampened his spirits, especially having to listen to their inane comments on the horse jumping competition. His marriage to Eunice was causing Andrew a lot of worry; he felt as her husband a commitment to her, but in what way eluded him. How he wished he had never set eyes on her or her family. He rarely saw her now, just about every fortnight or so.

Then Mr Gibson played another of his 'aces'; he invited Andrew to attend the local point-to-point meeting with the family. It was a race meeting for amateur owners and riders. Andrew resisted, but Mr Gibson again had his way and Andrew went along to the race meeting with them. There was a special enclosure for the members of the Point-to-Point Fellowship, and Mr Gibson and his party were directed here. It was the same clique, with the same back slapping and the same exaggerated laughs from the same weak quips.

This time it was even easier to walk away from them, as the enclosure was just roped off; it was just a matter of ducking under the ropes and he was with the ordinary race-goers. He met the twins Ernest and Patrick Spring. They were two farmers whom Andrew had helped on many occasions, when really he should have been at school. They had a few good natured jibes at him because of the Members' badge he had in his buttonhole, accusing him of mingling with the upper crust.

It was nearly time for the first race. Andrew asked the twins if they could suggest a horse that he could place a bet on. The twins looked at each other, and didn't answer, then they whispered to each other and Ernest said to Andrew:

'Save your money, Andy lad, we know a horse in the third race, the big race, it can't lose. We'll tell you its name nearer the time. We have a lot of money to go on it, and you can help us. If you look down the line of bookies you'll see there's six in the public part and three in the Members' enclosure. We have ninety pounds to go on this horse, and as all the bookies have limits as to how much they'll take, we need to get as much as we can on before the tic-tac man warns them and reduces the odds. We thought, as you have access to the Members' enclosure, you could take fifteen pounds of this money, and, of course, add all you've got of your own, and put it on with the bookies in the Members' enclosure. Mind you, it's all a matter of timing: you'll have to wait for my signal, and we'll all move in on the bookies together.'

Andrew stood with his mouth open, hardly able to believe what he was hearing. 'But I heard Mr Gibson say that Jakes Pride would win that race, that he's won it this last three years, and that he's so much of a certainty you'd have to put four shillings on to win one.'

Patrick took up the story. 'He won't beat our horse today, lad, and that is a certainty. We've been over to Ireland for him, he's a beauty. We had him at a point-to-point a fortnight ago, the one that was held at the Grange. He wasn't there to win, just a try out, and do you know, it was all our jockey could do to keep him back from winning. We were a bit worried as we watched him go, because if he had won we'd have had terrible trouble getting any sort of decent odds on him today.'

Andrew was excited, and could hardly wait for the big race. Patrick counted out the fifteen pounds to him, and he added three pounds of his own, which was all he had. He divided it into three pockets so that he could go to the three bookies and put the money on the horse without having any confusion counting it out.

After the second race was over, Ernest told him that the horse's name was Marsh Wanderer. Half an hour before the big race he told Andrew, 'It's time now to go back in the Members' enclosure. Stand down beside the bookies, near the rope. Watch for my signal, then run to the bookies. Don't make your move too soon; to get the best out of our bets, all three of us must go together. Off you go, now, and don't let us down.'

Andrew did as he was bid, and found a spot near the rope and near to the bookies. He could see Ernest quite clearly. The time seemed to drag over; the horses came out for the race, and he was beginning to think the twins had left it too late to place the bets. Then he received the long awaited signal. He ran to the first bookie and placed six pounds to win on Marsh Wanderer; it had odds of four to one. He ran to the second bookie and found him arguing with a client, so ran past him to the third bookie, and placed the same bet, again at four to one. He ran back to the second bookie to find the odds had shortened to three to one, but he had the bet placed just as the horses were lining up for the start of the race.

As the twins had foretold, Marsh Wanderer won easily. Feeling apprehensive, he walked down to the bookies, but he didn't need to worry, they were only too pleased to pay him out, for had Jakes Pride won, the favourite, they would have paid out a fortune. Nearly everyone on the course had put their money on him.

Andrew ducked under the ropes with eighty-four pounds in his pocket to hand over to the twins. They worked it out. Fourteen pounds was Andrew's share but they gave him sixteen, for doing so well; he had obtained better odds than they had. It was the most money he had ever had in his life. He was delighted; he'd had a wonderful afternoon. Even the trip home with the Gibsons didn't spoil it for him. He was in fact even more pleased, for by the Gibsons' talk they had all lost their money, most of it on Jakes Pride.

The following evening Mr Gibson called on Andrew and confirmed what the charade had been all about.

'Now look, lad, you must realise that this so-called marriage to my daughter is the biggest mistake you've ever made in your life. You must see that she's used to a style of life you could never provide her with. She's in a different class, poles apart is what you are, as different as chalk from cheese.'

Andrew could feel his hackles rising, but he kept his temper, as Mr Gibson carried on to say, 'I'm sure you want to be out of this so-called marriage as much as I want you out of it. I've been to see my solicitor, and according to him there were abnormalities that rendered the union just slightly illegal. If you will sign the appropriate letters and forms, he thinks he can have the marriage annulled. Will you do it?'

The feeling of relief outweighed Andrew's rising temper. At last there was a way out of his dilemma.

'I'll sign whatever you want,' he said. 'Now go and leave me in peace; I'll be glad to see the back of the whole lot of you.'

Andrew was able to settle to his work in a much better frame of mind. It was a tremendous weight off his shoulders, to think that he was finally to be rid of the Gibson family. An assortment of letters and forms were brought for him to sign; he couldn't read them, but never-the-less signed them.

Eventually, after a few months, he had a very official looking letter. Because of his lack of education, he couldn't read it, but had to take it to Lord John, who read it out to him. He looked a bit nonplussed when he heard some of the technical phrases. At the end of it all, Lord John put his hand on his shoulder and said, 'Your worries are over, lad, it means your marriage is ended!'

But it wasn't the end of his problems. That evening, when he returned from work, Mr and Mrs Gibson and Eunice were waiting for him. During the time Eunice and he had been together, they had accumulated an amount of decent furnishings: a good quality bedroom suite, a carpet, some silver cutlery, bone china crockery, a highly polished table and chairs and some tapestry. Mr Gibson was as usual the spokesperson. He told Andrew in no uncertain terms that Eunice wanted back what was hers. Andrew readily agreed, he didn't argue at all. 'Nearly everything that's in the house belongs to Eunice, and its only fair that she has it back.' They made arrangements for the furnishings to be collected the following Saturday.

Their mission being entirely successful, the Gibsons were happy to go on their way. Andrew laughed to himself; there would be hardly anything left in the house, but it was only fair, everything had been presents from Eunice's friends or relations, or from her 'bottom drawer'. It was only right that she had them back.

Two of the Gibson workers came with a large horse-drawn, four-wheel flat wagon. They were accompanied by Eunice's two brothers, both riding their hunters. They stood back with a smirk on their faces as the men carried out the furnishings. Normally Andrew would have pitched in and helped, but as it was beneath the two brothers to help, Andrew contented himself by just standing there watching as they carried the pieces out.

As a present from his grandmother Andrew had been given an ornately carved, highly polished Oriental blanket box. Eunice had been particularly fond of it. The men carried it from the house with the intention of loading it on to the wagon, but Andrew wasn't prepared to let her have it, so he told the men to put it back. The two brothers were not suited; the smirks were replaced by scowls. They didn't say anything, and eventually the load was roped and the wagon moved off.

Andrew smiled when he walked into the house. He was left with what he started with: a rickety bed, two kitchen chairs, a table that had to be spragged under one leg, a length of coco-matting for the floor, the two-burner paraffin oil stove to cook on, and the ornately carved, Oriental blanket box.

That night he sat by the fire and thought things over. It was like waking up from a nightmare, a period in his life that he could begin to forget. He could settle himself and concentrate on his work. He cheered himself with the thought that he had twenty-four pounds hidden away: the sixteen pounds he had won at the point-to-point plus another eight pounds he had saved from his wages. He planned to buy himself some home comforts, and an easy-chair was high on his list.

But it wasn't all over. The next Saturday afternoon, he was working on a fence when he saw a pony and trap trotting up toward his house. He ran over the field to find Eunice's two brothers, half drunk, carrying his blanket box out to the pony and trap. Andrew was furious: not only were they stealing from him, they had broken into his house to do it. Not that it took much breaking into, as the key was on a string hanging behind the woodshed door. Andrew ordered them to put it back and threatened them with the police if they ever came near his house again. They put the box down and the elder brother spoke to him. His voice was slurred, but still arrogant.

'What does a dolt like you want a thing like this for? You're as ignorant as the pigs you look after.'

Andrew advanced on him, rage rising. The younger brother came to meet him, and called him an idle, unknowing, indolent clod-hopper. He threatened Andrew with the hiding of his life. His fists were flailing like windmills as he approached Andrew, who couldn't resist it. He stepped back two paces, and the younger brother, being half drunk, lost his balance and came stumbling forward. Andrew caught him with a beautiful right with his hard bony fist, and the man went down as though pole-axed. He didn't make any effort to get back on his feet, but just lay there, shouting profanities. The elder brother then approached Andrew, a murderous look on his face. Without a word he laid into him with the ivory-handled riding crop. Andrew had no defence against it, the blows rained on him, every one drawing blood. He could feel his senses slipping from him, as he backed toward the fence. In desperation he grabbed one of the three-cornered palings. The nails were weak, it came away in his hand, and with the last of his strength he hit the elder brother with it. It finished the fight, as the fence paling broke the elder brother's cheekbone and knocked out four of his teeth.

For Andrew's part in the fight, the local policeman put him in a cell for the night. Three weeks later he had to appear before the magistrates, and was dismayed to see that the Chief Magistrate was one of the back-slapping clique he had seen at the Hunt Ball, the County Show and the point-to-point. Andrew was shown no mercy; they wouldn't even listen to his side of the event. He was sentenced to three years in prison, while the two brothers walked away scot free.

For Andrew a more agonizing punishment could not have been devised. Being confined in prison triggered off some sort of mental reaction in him, very much like school had been to him, but from the prison there was no escape. At a later time, his aversion to being enclosed would probably have been recognised as a disease and allowances made, but not so then. He fretted and brooded so much that his appetite and confidence left him. The only thing on the plus side to come out of it was that one of the older prisoners took an interest in him and taught him the basics in reading and writing.

Andrew served twenty-six months in the prison and was released. If he had stayed longer he would probably have died. His weight had dropped from over eleven stones to under five. He was a mental and physical wreck when he returned to his parents' home.

In the relatively short time that he had been out of circulation, a lot of changes had come about. Lord John had retired, and Andrew's job and home were no longer available to him, although Lord John did still own the farms. He was pleased to learn that the Gibson family had gone bankrupt. The farm, the hunters and the fine life-style were no longer at hand, and the father and Eunice's two brothers were having to bear the humiliation of looking for work, work they were ill-equipped to handle.

Andrew, at home, did eat a little better, and his health improved slightly, but he too dreaded the prospect of looking for work. He had been out of prison for about a fortnight when Lord John called on him.

'How are you, young Andrew? I was sorry to hear how badly you've been getting away with things. I'm sorry I couldn't keep your job open for you, it's 'cos time marches on. I'm no longer a young man and I'm looking forward to a touch of the easy life for my last few years. Now then, enough of that, this is what I have come to see you about. You know old Edward Clough, he's on Beck End Farm; it belongs to me, you know. Well, he's been to see me, he wants to pack it in. Between you and me, he should have done it twenty years ago, he's been past it for easily that long, consequently the place has gone to rack and ruin. It's in a terrible state, both land and buildings. Basically it's a decent place, two hundred and fifty acres it is, forty acres of that woodland. Do you fancy taking it on as a tenant? The rent is only a pound an acre.'

Andrew explained to Lord John that, although he had plenty of experience on the practical side, he didn't understand the money side of farming, and besides he was broke, he didn't have any money.

'Look, Andrew lad, I know you're the man to do it. I've seen the way you work, and if you need advice, I'll keep you right with the economics of it. I'm even prepared to let you have it rent free for the first couple of years, because of the dilapidated state of the farm. I'm even prepared to loan you a hundred or two, to help you get started. Let's not say any more about it at the minute. Just come over to my house in the morning, and we'll look it over. What do you say?'

Andrew agreed.

Lord John's parting words were, 'Old Edward wants out as soon as possible, so there's no reason why you shouldn't take over immediately.'

Andrew's rehabilitation started instantaneously, and for the first time since he had been put in jail, his mental attitude was positive. He ate and enjoyed his supper, he slept well, and rose early. After breakfast he made his way over to Lord John's house. From the moment he stepped onto Becks End Farm, he knew it was right for him. He looked at the dilapidated house and buildings, the overgrown hedges, the silted up ditches and drains, the hungry look of the fields, and the weed-strewn meadows. He saw only potential; his plans for the farm were already building in his brain. He knew he would soon rebuild his strength and put the farm to his satisfaction. He was thinking 'soon', even though his plans were taking at least ten years from his life.

Lord John was as good as his word, and loaned Andrew two hundred pounds. The ordeal of his jail sentence over and the pattern of his life set, he was able to turn his mind to everyday things. His first concern was for his blanket box, the one that had caused him so much trouble. He walked over to the ill-fated house in which he had once lived. He asked the tenants if they had any idea what had happened to it, and the lady of the house answered him:

'It's such a lovely piece, we knew you'd come back for it. We've kept it safe for you, it's in our bedroom. When would you like to take it?'

'If it's all the same to you, I'd like to take it this afternoon, as soon as I can find something to transport it with.'

His mother's next door neighbour had a hand-cart which he borrowed. In his weakened state it was hard going, over two miles to his ex-house, but he got there and loaded the blanket box. As soon as he was out of sight he stopped and opened it. It hadn't been touched, and was the same inside as he had left it, with just one white blanket. He removed the blanket and put it carefully on the hand-cart. The box had a double bottom; he removed one of the boards and found his twenty-four pounds savings still intact. He was going to need it. Two hundred and twenty-four pounds wasn't much to finance a farm, but he would stretch it as far as it would go.

He was advised to open a bank account by Lord John, which he did. Then he started in earnest on the farm. He bought an old Shire horse, a coup cart and a dozen heifer calves, which all cost him his first hundred pounds. He moved into the broken down farmhouse and began to make his plans reality. It took the ten years to lick the farm into anything like shape, the first five years being the worst. For those first five years he denied himself everything; he only slept and worked. He had neither friends nor entertainment of any sort.

Andrew's efforts were rewarded. Slowly he built up a turnover, and was able to repay Lord John, buy better stock, pay his rent, and invest in two good Shire horses and some labour saving implements. He shrewdly bought artificial manures. All this plus the buildings he had improved to increase his efficiency, all added up to make money. His personal needs were small, so he was able to afford to have an employee. He had a succession of men, but none of them lasted long, as he expected too much of them, imagining they should keep pace with him. He had turned himself into a very successful farmer.

Andrew did get married again, to a local attractive girl who was about five or six years older than he. She was a pleasant, friendly girl; she was good for him, and, while she was with him, brought him a great deal of happiness. Unfortunately she wasn't too healthy and her heart gave out on her whilst in her mid-forties. There were no children from the marriage.

Andrew was in his late fifties when he was presented with an instant daughter and grand-daughter. Around nine o'clock at night he always had a last look round his stock, when he would shake up their bedding and, if they had cleaned up their food, he would give them an extra bite of hay. It was a routine he had followed every winter night for more than thirty years. He thought he caught a glimpse of light in the trees at the far side of the field opposite the house. He stood a few minutes, but failed to see the light again. 'Ah,' he thought to himself, 'I must be seeing things,' and decided to return to the warmth of the house.

He sat by the fire, but couldn't settle himself. It was a cold windy night, he didn't want to go out again. But it was on his mind, he knew he wouldn't sleep. He kept turning it over in his mind: could it be poachers or, worse still, sheep stealers? These things were going on in the district.

He pulled his boots and coat back on, tucked his twelve-bore shotgun under his arm, and made his way over to the wood. He had the shock of his life to find a young girl, alone in a tiny car. It was the interior light that he had seen through the trees. She was in labour, and in great difficulties. Andrew had attended too many difficult births to his animals, over the years, not to know the signs. Even though it was a cold raw night, and she only lightly dressed, the sweat ran down her face from her unproductive efforts. He hid his twelve-bore shotgun in the undergrowth and covered her with his heavy coat. He talked to her soothingly, telling her to save her exertions till he could take her to hospital, where she would receive professional help.

Andrew had never driven a car in his life, but he managed to start it, turn it round, and then drive it five miles in first gear to the hospital. He stayed at the hospital until the early hours of the morning, and was pleased to hear that she had been delivered of a baby girl. They were both well, and he was allowed a peep at them from the door of the ward. The baby lay peaceably in a cot; the mother, heavily sedated, lay in bed oblivious to the world.

Andrew returned to the hospital the following afternoon at visiting time, to see how they both were. He was embarrassed by the welcome he received. The girl threw her arms around him, buried her head in his shoulder and cried her eyes out for a good ten minutes. In that time she must have thanked him a dozen times.

'I hope you don't mind, but I've told them all here that you are my uncle,'

'Mind, I don't mind, in fact I'm proud to be your uncle.'

He was her only visitor, and he never missed a visiting period in the nine days she was confined in the hospital. In that time they learned a little of each other's history. Her name was Eve Blackwell; she was a Canadian, studying at the University. She was a young looking eighteen-year-old and unmarried. The father of the child, another student, had disclaimed the baby and dumped the mother when he had learned she was pregnant. She had told her mother and father, who were working

71

in London, of her predicament. They belonged to a fanatical religious group and had disowned her, 'washed their hands of her' as Eve herself had put it. They had even stopped sending her money. She had not been able to pay her lodgings; she owed her landlady twenty-two pounds. She hadn't told another soul as, being quite a plump girl, she had been able to hide her condition. When she had felt labour pains, she had taken her professor's car, without his permission, and, without any direction, had just driven. Luckily her journey had ended in the woods on Andrew's farm.

When her time came to leave the hospital she asked Andrew if she could stay at the farm for a week or two, till she could get her life back together and make a decision about the baby girl, whether to have her adopted, or perhaps find some sort of work that would allow her to keep the child. Andrew was delighted to agree; he knew from the way she looked at the baby, and how she handled her, that she had no intention of giving her up. He had seen this same situation so many times before. When a daughter became pregnant, the initial reaction of the family was invariably hostile, but at the end of the day, they always capitulated and rallied behind their hapless daughters. He felt sure it would be the same for Eve, and that when her mother and father were in possession of all the facts, they would relent and welcome their daughter back into the fold.

With Eve, and the baby whom she had named Rowena, settled at the farm, Andrew made the journey into town. The fact that no one knew what had become of her was clearly bothering Eve, and to put her mind at rest he called first on her professor. Andrew told him what had happened to her, and was able to enlighten him on what had happened to his car. It was still standing in the hospital grounds, where Andrew had left it; the police had been unable to find it. Andrew left the professor standing scratching his head, mouth open, with a glazed look in his eye. Secondly he called on her landlady, an old, money-grabbing termagant who wasn't in the least interested in what had happened to Eve. He offered her the twenty-two pounds that was owed to her, but she twisted, it wasn't enough. She could have earned an extra three pounds by letting it to some one else, had she known the circumstances. Andrew paid her the twenty-five pounds and, without another word, turned his back on her.

That evening the two discussed the possibility of a reconciliation with her parents. Eve insisted that it was pointless making any approach to them; she said she knew only too well that when they made a decision, there was never any possibility of them reneging. Andrew was equally convinced that when they knew the full facts of what had happened, and what a beautiful grand-daughter they had, they would be only too pleased to have her back with them. Andrew talked her over into letting him go to London and personally tell them the whole story.

On the Saturday morning he caught the early morning train to King's Cross. Eve had written her parents' address on the back of an envelope. On leaving the station, he approached a cab, and read out the address to the driver. It was an address in Mayfair, and he didn't realise how fashionable the area was until the cabby said to him, 'Cor blimey, me old china, ya gonna be among the toffs to-day an no mistake, eh!'

To say his meeting with the Blackwells was 'pert', was putting it mildly. He rang the bell, and he was answered by a maid.

'Yes?' she said in a stern voice.

'Could I speak to Mr or Mrs Blackwell, please.'

'In connection with what?' she said in the same tone.

'It's personal; tell them I'm from up north, and it's to do with their daughter.'

Mrs Blackwell came to the door. Andrew was just starting to tell her of Eve when Mr Blackwell came out; obviously he had been listening to the conversation. He stepped between Andrew and his wife.

'The girl you are describing is a sinner! and is of no consequence to us, so if you please, sir, we are very busy, we are packing to return to Canada. Please leave, and don't bother us again.'

If Andrew had been among his own people he would have had a few choice words to say to Mr Blackwell but, considering his situation, he could only say, 'It's your loss,' and turn his back and leave them.

One of the few books he had ever read had featured Buckingham Palace, and in his mind he never believed that such a place existed. When he found a cab, he asked the driver if he would take him to see the Palace, then on to King's Cross station. It was just as it had been described, magnificent. His trip to London hadn't been completely wasted; he now knew Buckingham Palace really existed. He found a café near the station, and had his lunch, then looked round the nearby shops. There were crowds of people about, yet Andrew had never felt so alone in his life. No one spoke to him or looked him in the eye. Everyone seemed to have a purpose and wouldn't be deviated. He was pleased when the time came to board the train.

On his way home he turned the situation over in his mind. He had never met such parsimonious, unforgiving people in his life as Eve's mother and father. He decided he would offer Eve the chance to stay with him permanently at the farm.

It was an opportunity heaven-sent for Eve, as she could keep the baby with her. In return she would help Andrew as much as she could; she would keep house, and do as much paper work for him as she could. The arrangement was equally good for both of them. Eve was a lovely natured girl, and they soon drifted into a father and daughter relationship. As Rowena progressed and started to talk, she called Andrew Grandad. It pleased him no end, and his household was happier than it had ever been.

As it had been for Lord John, time was marching on for Andrew. Lord John was long dead, but Andrew still thought a lot of him, and how good he had been to him. The phrases he used often came into Andrew's head, the one ever more coming to the fore being when he had spoken of old Edward Clough, the previous tenant.

'He should have packed in years ago, he's been past it that long, you know, he's let the place go to rack and ruin.'

Andrew, now in his mid sixties, was feeling the effects of his age; twinging rheumatic pains were making it difficult to get started on a job, and his enthusiasm for his work was lessening. He didn't want to be spoken of as Edward Clough had been, and most of all he wanted Eve set up in a business that she could manage, that would keep her and Rowena comfortable after he had passed on.

Lord John's descendants were keen to have the farms back into the family. They had hired an unscrupulous agent to dispossess the tenants who had used the ploy of threatening to take them to court, to make them pay for dilapidations to their farms, an action which could quite easily take all the money they had. Every farm has faults that could be put down to dilapidation: broken gates and fences, walls in poor condition, silted up ditches, damaged drains, noxious weeds in pastures, and numerous other things; they were all the tenants' responsibilities.

The plan had worked with all the tenants except Andrew. The agent had looked round all the farms and had compiled a list of faults, which had frightened the farmers into giving up their tenancies without any compensation whatever. Andrew was ready to retire, but there was no way he was leaving because of any threats from the agent. He wasn't going to be intimidated. When the time came to go to court, the hearing didn't last half an hour. The agent read out how the farm, in his opinion, should be, and how much, in his estimation, it would cost to have the farm put to his liking. Andrew, however, still had the original letter he had received from Lord John, which clearly stated the condition of the farm when Andrew had accepted the tenancy. The judge read it, found in favour of Andrew, stopped the hearing, and ordered that all Andrew's costs be met and that he shouldn't be harassed any further.

The following week Andrew had a letter from the agent requesting a meeting. Andrew told him at the meeting that he was ready to retire, and that he would give up the farm, but only if he were offered the proper compensation. In a short time a deal was made, and Andrew left the farm a relatively wealthy man. The compensation money was enough to buy a house and the newsagent's business, leaving the bulk of his savings intact. He made no secret of the fact that when the time came this money too was for Eve and Rowena, his adopted daughter and grand-daughter.

Charlie felt a bit guilty, not crossing the road for a chat with Andrew, but this wasn't the day for it.

CHAPTER 11

During his sister Hannah's illness, Charlie's life changed dramatically: he started courting. Lilly Ransome had been Hannah's best friend from school days, and they had been regular visitors to each other's houses over the years. Charlie had always been friendly with Lilly, but couldn't quite say at what point the friendship had deepened. Charlie often thought about it, and concluded that it was probably at Lilly's works outing that romance had developed between them. The arrangement was that Hannah would accompany her, but with her illness progressing it wasn't possible. Charlie was asked to take her place.

It was a wonderful day out, to the local seaside resort in two private coaches. Everyone was friendly, the sun shone all day, and even though Lilly had all her work friends with her, she still gave all her attention to Charlie. They sat in the sun on the sand and watched youngsters build sand castles. They took off their shoes and socks and paddled in the sea. Lunch was booked for them all, in a room at an hotel. In the afternoon they rode on the roundabouts till they were giddy, then played the penny-in-the-slot machines, to try and win their fortunes. On the coach going home, Lilly put her head on his shoulder and, with a smile of contentment, slept most of the way.

On the evenings when Lilly visited Hannah and had a meal with them, usually two or three times a week, Charlie would meet her at the works gate and, if it was a fine night, they'd walk arm in arm home. On a wet night they'd take the bus. Later in the evening, after the visit, Charlie would walk Lilly to her own home. They would always talk for five minutes on her doorstep, and the best part of it all was a warm kiss good-night. It always left Charlie with a top-of-the-world feeling.

Had Charlie been left to his own devices, the romance would not have progressed very quickly, but he was coerced into speeding things up by his mother and sick sister. He came in from work one evening to hear the beginning of a conversation between them. Hannah, ignoring Charlie, said to her mother, 'You know, Mam, they've got a new maintenance man at Lilly's factory. By all accounts he's a real heart-throb, a right tasty dish. All the girls are mad keen on him. But he's only got eyes for Lilly, he's pestering her every day for a date.'

Charlie left the room to wash and shave. Hannah's words were echoing in his head, and jealousy was creeping into his heart, for he had come to think of Lilly as his girl. He should have 'smelled a rat' when he returned to the room, as the conversation hadn't moved on. His mother was speaking.

'What did you say his name was?'

'Ooh, Mam, even his name sends shivers down your spine. It's Charlton Jefferies, isn't it romantic?'

'Eeh, Hannah, it is that, and by, Lilly's a real nice lass, she deserves someone who will be good to her; she has the makings of a good wife for some lucky chap. And you know, Hannah, she's coming to an age when she needs an understanding with someone, so she can plan her life.'

'Yes, Mam, that's true.'

Charlie had heard enough; he made an excuse and left the room. He was churning up inside. 'Charlton Jefferies,' he thought to himself, 'I'll give him a run for his money; keen on Lilly, is he? We'll see about that.'

Over the next few weeks, Charlie took particular care with his appearance. He kept his hair in good trim, he washed and shaved regularly, he dressed tidily, and he courted Lilly. It paid off for him. They soon had an 'understanding'; he didn't buy a ring, but they were engaged. They each had commitments at their respective homes, so there wouldn't be any chance of marriage in the immediate future, but they enjoyed making plans.

The talk of war with Germany was becoming ever more serious, resulting in ever more pressure for production in the foundry where Charlie worked. The same was happening at Lilly's factory. The extra hours they each had to work lessened the time they had to spend with each other, but they made the best of the time that was available.

Charlie had a surprise one evening. Lilly was waiting for him at the foundry gates.

'Charlie, love, you'll just have to come with me. You know the Bottom Colliery has been building new houses, nearer to the Colliery. Well, they are selling the houses that they own in Beech Street. What happens is, as the families move into the new houses, they wait until there's four or five of them empty and they auction them off. They are perfectly good houses, and only make about sixty or seventy pounds each. Please, Charlie, come and look.'

She was so bright eyed and excited, he couldn't have said no. It was only a quarter of a mile or so to Beech Street, ten minutes walking time. Lilly talked of the houses all the time while they made the journey, about how well built they were, how central the houses were for each of their jobs, ideal for when they were married.

When they arrived there was a clerk present from the estate agents who were conducting the auction. He was very helpful, and showed them round the four houses that were for sale. He explained to them how the auction worked. They only needed ten per cent of the purchase price, to be paid 'on the fall of the hammer', then they had a month in which to pay the remainder. He also explained to them that the office ran a loan scheme: they kept the deeds of the property and the purchaser paid monthly. When the debt was paid, the deeds would be handed over. As Charlie and Lilly each had good jobs he didn't see there being any problem.

After looking over all four houses, Lilly decided she liked number 32 best, and that was the one they should try for.

'Ah now,' said the clerk, ' a little more advice for you. In my experience in these sorts of auctions, the earlier lots make less money than the later ones, and if you look at the schedule you will see that number 32 is last to be sold. Why not have another look at one of the earlier ones?'

They did have another look, and decided to try for number 14. Before they left the clerk gave them some more advice:

'To buy one of these houses is a wise move; do you know, after your deposit is paid, the repayments on the loan can be less than the rent you would pay for a similar dwelling.'

Lilly could talk of nothing else all evening. Charlie was pleased that the auction was to be the next evening, as the tension was telling on him already and the whole thing had only been with him for these last few hours. If, as Lilly had said, the houses only made sixty, seventy, or even eighty pounds, the deposit wouldn't be a difficulty. With the overtime Charlie was working his wages had risen considerably. He had nearly twenty pounds, and Lilly too had money saved.

They met the following evening. Lilly's enthusiasm hadn't lessened. The auction was to be held in the upstairs room of the White Swan. There were only about twenty people present, and at six thirty prompt, the advertised time of the sale, the auctioneer, a stoutish, short man, stood up on a platform and read out the conditions of sale. Charlie was pleased to hear him say, the same as his clerk: ten per cent deposit, the remainder within twenty-eight days.

Charlie's legs had turned to jelly as the auctioneer described number 14, the first lot. He seemed to go on for ever; how Charlie wished that he would hurry and finish the descriptions, and start taking bids. There was a hush in the room when he asked for the first bid.

'Can I have eighty pounds?' There were no takers as he looked round. 'Seventy then?' Still no takers. 'Someone start me, sixty, say.'

Someone in the gathering said, 'Forty.'

'Come on, people, that's an insult, not a bid.' The auctioneer was laughing. 'But still, if that's what you want to start, I can see you are going to make me work for my money. I will take bids of five pounds till we get to a more realistic figure.' The bidding rose quickly to fifty-five pounds. Lilly gave Charlie a nudge; he raised his hand.

'Right, sir, I have you at sixty.'

For what seemed an age, the bidding rested at Charlie's bid of sixty pounds. Then the auctioneer said, 'I'll take ones now. Any more bids?'

The bidding rose to sixty-six pounds; it was Charlie's bid.

'Sixty-six pounds, this is your last chance; make no mistake, I'm selling it.'

He brought his hammer down, looked at Charlie, and said, 'Yours, sir; come up and speak to my clerk.'

Charlie handed twenty pounds to the clerk, fifteen of it his, the other five Lilly's. They made arrangements to call at the office the following day, to arrange a loan for the remainder.

'It will be a pleasure, sir; if you see me I'll deal with it myself for you. Now, just listen to the auctioneer for a moment; he's selling number

25; it's a worse house than the one you have just bought.'

They listened; the bids were already up to seventy pounds, and still rising.

'Didn't I tell you, the first one is nearly always the cheapest.'

As predicted by the auctioneer's clerk, the loan for the remainder of the purchase price was easy. It would be paid off over five years, and worked out to be a few shillings a week, less than its rental value. Because of their commitments, they didn't have the time they would have liked to spend on the house, but what time they had together was spent there, making a start in putting it to their liking and making plans for their future.

Hannah was now a big worry to her mother and to Charlie. She was deteriorating week by week. It was heartbreaking waiting for the inevitable.

One evening, shortly after they had bought the house, came a night Charlie often thought of with a grin on his face. It was cold and windy, with blustery rain. He was to meet Lilly at the end of her shift and see her home. He arrived at the factory gates about quarter of an hour early, and took shelter behind the wall. The gate-man called him over, having recognised him.

'Take yourself over to the canteen, lad, it's too bad a night to stand about outside. Mavis'll give you a cup of tea. You'll not miss your girl, they always come out through the canteen.' Charlie didn't need a second bidding; he was over like a shot into the warmth of the canteen. The woman behind the counter, whom he took to be Mavis, poured him a cup of tea as he walked through the door. Charlie thanked her and sat down beside a chap whom he remembered from the works' outing. He had been chatting with him for about five minutes when an oldish man, at least seventy years old, looked into the canteen. He had a vacant look to him. He called over to the chap Charlie was talking to: 'Have you seen anything of Joseph?'

'No, Charlton, he hasn't been in here.'

His question answered, he turned and walked out.

'Is that Charlton Jefferies, your new maintenance man?' asked Charlie.

The man laughed and said, 'New maintenance man; he's been here twenty years or more. It's Charlton Jefferies, but he's not exactly all there, if you know what I mean.' The man could hardly stop himself laughing. 'Maintenance man, he's sweeper-up, an' it's all he can manage to do that; he's only about tenpence ha'penny to the shilling, you know.'

Charlie was grinning now. He'd had a good look at Charlton when he had stood in the doorway. His hair hadn't been trimmed for months, nor had a comb through it. He had a permanent drip on his nose that kept his heavily nicotined moustache constantly wet. His neck and ears were ingrained with dirt. His shirt, waistcoat and trousers were filthy and riddled with cigarette burns. He had looked dreadful. The chap Charlie was chatting to nudged him and said, 'It pays not to get downwind of him either.'

Charlie, still grinning, thought to himself, 'Send shivers down the girls' spines, will he? but it will not be with romantic notions.'

Going home in the bus, Lilly was a bit nonplussed; she couldn't understand why Charlie kept grinning. She shook her head when he wouldn't enlighten her.

Hannah's illness, and eventual death, took thirteen months. It showed how tough she had been; the pain she had suffered must have been horrendous. Even after she had lost consciousness, she had lasted a week. It wasn't a terribly sad funeral, for although it wasn't said, everyone recognised her death as a great relief from her suffering. The vicar's words: 'A long illness bravely born,' seemed to say it all.

Events seemed to be stacking up against Charlie and Lilly being able to make anything of the house they had bought. Just a week or two after the funeral, there was a tragedy at Charlie's works. There were four of them who always worked together: the foreman, who had known Charlie's father, two workmates, Bert Hughes and Jim White, and Charlie. They were to shift a load of sand, to make way for some new castings. They had completed the same job dozens of times. Halfway down the shop, Bert said to Charlie, 'That's a bad shovel you've got hold of to-day, Charlie. It nips your hand. I had it the other day and it took a piece out of my palm.'

'I'll go back and get another.'

Charlie heard a bang and a lot of shouting and hurried straight back to where he had left his workmates. There had been a sealed hydraulic cylinder in the scrap metal that was being recycled. It had exploded with the heat and had blown out the side of the vessel that was holding the semi-molten metal. Charlie's workmates had all been badly burned in the accident.

The foreman had suffered the worst of the blast, and in the first week it was thought he would die, but he was a tough old stick. He would be disfigured, but he would survive, though he would never be able to return to work. His other two workmates would be in hospital for several weeks, and possibly they too would never return to the foundry. Everyone said how lucky Charlie had been to escape the accident, yet he felt guilty somehow. He felt as if he had cheated, by not being involved, and felt decidedly uncomfortable at work.

CHAPTER 12

Charlie pulled out of his day-dreams with a start. Even after all the years, the accident still stirred something in him. He found himself gazing at a small house, right next door to what had been an imposing, double fronted shop. It had not always been a house. In Charlie's youth, a wooden shed had stood on the site. It had belonged to Sydney Barker, a jobbing builder with a labourer named Pat, an Irishman. They seemed to be inseparable, and they always had with them a three-wheeled hand-cart. The loads they carried on it were unbelievable. They were two characters. Sydney looked like a weasel; Pat was tall and thin, not a picking of fat on either of them. Why they stayed together was a mystery. They had argued continually; if Sydney said an article was light red, Pat would say it was dark pink.

Charlie remembered them with affection. To the kids in the neighbourhood, Charlie included, they had been like two pantomime characters, the source of much amusement. Generations of kids had followed them, mimicking Sydney by shouting, 'More lime, and a brick, Pat!'

Eventually Sydney passed away, and Pat made his way home to Ireland. Sydney's descendants didn't have any interest in his business, and the shed and the site on which it stood were sold, the purchaser electing to clear the site and build a house on it.

Sydney's philosophy had always been that a job was not only done, but seen to be done, consequently he had used a lot of paint in the finishing of his jobs. He had kept in the shed all that had remained of the paint. When it was demolished all the part-used paint tins were thrown out and Charlie's friend Fred Harding, the one whose funeral he had just attended, had gathered up all the discarded paint tins in his barrow and taken them home. Charlie had called round, and had been taken to see them.

'Fred, what are you going to do with all the paint?'

'I'm going to paint my pigeon loft, will you give me a hand?'

'But how on earth are you going to do it, there's not enough of any one colour to go anywhere near covering it?'

'I thought we could just mix them all together; after all, I'm not interested what colour it turns out, just so long as I keep the weather out.'

They made arrangements for Charlie to call round on the Saturday afternoon, when they prised the lids from all the paint tins. Most of them were nearly empty. They poured what there was into an enamelled bowl; there were all colours, black, white, green, blue, red and yellow, and all in various shades. When all mixed together they turned into a dirty, greyish colour. Charlie and Fred, each with a brush, took less than an hour to finish the job.

Charlie had tea with Fred and his wife and sat and talked for an hour or so, preparing to go to the White Swan for a glass of beer and a game of dominoes. There was a frenzied knocking at Fred's back door. It was a neighbour, Portsmouth Joe, from a few doors down the street. When he was agitated he had a bad stammer.

'Fred, c-c-come, and s-s-s-see ya p-pigeon d-d-ducket.'

'What's wrong with it?' said Fred.

Portsmouth Joe couldn't get any more words out, he was tugging Fred's sleeve, leading him towards the garden. Charlie followed close behind. They all stood at the top of the garden and gawped at the pigeon loft. The mixture of paint had taken on a luminous quality. The loft was glowing in the darkening. It was a most unnatural sight. Portsmouth Joe broke the silence.

'It's b-b-better t-than the the Taj Mahal b-by m-m-m-moonlight.'

It was more than a week before it lost its luminosity, and in that time it was the most viewed, most talked about subject in the neighbourhood. Recalling the incident brought a grin to Charlie's face, and a lump into his throat.

CHAPTER 13

S ydney Barker's was one of the few where Charlie had not been a customer. His gaze shifted to the double fronted shop that was next door to what had been Sydney Barker's shed. It was tatty now with a sign on it which read, 'For sale, or to let'. The name of the previous owner could still be read, even though an attempt had been made to obliterate it with a thin coat of brown paint. Before his death the shop had belonged to William Makepeace. 'Purveyor of fine foods' had been written across the window. William Makepeace had been the town grocer, and Charlie, along with everyone else in the town, had been a customer of his. He had run the shop with the help of his wife and her sister. To Charlie, when he had been younger, it seemed as if they had been there for ever. He was a funny little man, who always seemed to be dominated by the two sisters. He didn't often serve in the shop, the two sisters did that, but he was forever busy, weighing out butter, sugar, potatoes and other groceries, for it was always delivered in bulk in those days. William did a delivery service for his not-so-sprightly customers, and employed two older school boys. They delivered groceries on a bicycle with a large basket attached over the front wheel.

One of these lads, Stanley Connor, had done very well for himself. He was now Chief Superintendent in the local police force, in charge of a dozen or so officers. He had formed quite a friendship with the grocer, and called at the shop every time he was in the vicinity. William Makepeace and his wife, although they always looked out of place, were invited to all the family 'dos', that Stanley Connor and his wife held.

William Makepeace's sister-in-law and Stanley Connor each had a daughter, of about the same age. They attended a very high class private girls' school, East Oakenton High School for Girls. Wealthy parents from all over the country paid for their daughters to be taught there.

Kathleen Connor and Lilian Parker, who was William Makepeace's niece, were firm friends. They had very different characters: Kathleen tendered to be a bit flighty and her concentration often wandered, whereas Lilian was a much steadier, more studious girl. They were good for each other; their friendship made a balance in their lives: the right amount of study, to the right amount of enjoyment. The two girls were regular visitors to each other's houses, where they would listen to music, talk, or compare notes on their school work. Lilian, whenever she had time, would come and help in the shop. Kathleen on occasions would call to see Lilian there.

Lilian's Uncle William was the bane of Kathleen's life. She blushed easily, and William could always find some comment to embarrass her. It was the same for her at the Connor family functions. William and his wife were always invited by her father, and she dreaded their coming. Not only for the embarrassment to her personally, she also felt disconcerted because they were so out of place against their more socially acceptable guests. She had a feeling that her mother thought more or less along the same lines. She was, of course, much too much of a lady to mention it. Besides, everyone, including the Lord Mayor, called her father 'Sir'. William called him 'Young Stan', and her father accepted it. She felt sure it rankled her mother.

The two girls eventually left school and, because of the high regard for East Oakenton High School for Girls, each was able to secure a very good job, with prospects of executive positions as they gained experience. In their different lines of work their paths divided, but they kept up their friendship.

Being working girls meant big changes in both of the girls' lives. The one thing Kathleen would have loved to change was, however, beyond her. Lilian's Uncle William was still invited by her father to all the family occasions. It seemed that he was the proverbial cross she had to bear. It wouldn't have mattered so much if Lilian's Uncle William had fitted in with their social circle; he didn't, his education was lacking, if all the tailors in Savile Row were to get together, they couldn't have dressed him tidily, and he wore boots. The very thought of it sent shudders through her.

The time came for Kathleen's first date. Frank English had asked her to accompany him to a dinner and dance in Town. Frank's father was high up in local government, and the family were well thought of in the area. Kathleen's mother and father readily agreed to the date. Everything seemed perfect, but she had a feeling of foreboding; she knew something would go wrong, and she knew Lilian's Uncle William would have something to do with it.

The evening came round and, as her feelings had predicted, Uncle William and his wife were visiting. Everything was going so well. Frank was the perfect gentleman; he had brought flowers for her mother, explained where he was taking Lilian, and at what time to expect them back. It was all so formal, and agreeable. They were walking across the hall towards the front door when Uncle William spoke. He tended to be a trifle deaf, and this made his voice shrill and penetrating.

'Mind, ah expect you two to behave yourselves, ah don't want to hear of any hankey-pankey.'

Kathleen felt her body stiffen, the hair on the back of her neck bristled, and the colour in her cheeks rose. She quickened her step and strode through the front door. Poor Frank tried to keep up, and fell down the two steps onto the garden path. He bounced back up, like a rubber ball, so quickly that Kathleen only caught a glimpse of what had happened. He was grinning like a Cheshire cat.

For Kathleen the evening was ruined. Frank's highly polished shoes were scuffed, his immaculately pressed trousers were a mess, they had great white patches on the knees, and one sleeve of his jacket was soiled. Frank tried to assure her that it didn't matter what had happened to him. Kathleen blamed Uncle William, and murderous thoughts wouldn't leave her mind.

The next big event in Kathleen's life was her eighteenth birthday. Her parents had organised a party for her and, as usual, Uncle William and his wife were invited. Kathleen had passed her driving test just a few weeks previously. She boasted she was a better driver than most, to all who were in her social circle. Kathleen and her mother had worked on her father for weeks, and had at last talked him into buying her the brand new sports car that had stood in a high class showroom. She had looked at it and sat in it on numerous occasions over the last couple of weeks. It was pricey, £2,300, as against the normal 'bread and butter' car that sold at about £800, but she felt that the sports car was the one for her. At her party she proudly told all her guests of the wonderful present she was to have. They were all delighted for her, and congratulated her on being so lucky as to be the owner of such a vehicle. Everyone, that is, except Uncle William, who with one sentence ruined it all for her. When told, he said to her father, 'Have ya come clean out of your tree, Young Stan?'

That was the end of her aspirations to the sports car. After that, all he would agree to buying was a second-hand 'bread and butter' car. She seethed with anger and frustration at the time, and very quickly the whole episode turned into an embarrassment she didn't like to think about.

She used the car for everything, even the shortest journeys, such as into town, where she could just as easily have walked. She soon found that her boast was very true; she was a better driver than most. She could drive faster, manoeuvre better, and generally handle a car in a far superior manner. She also found she had a power not available to the masses. She was not only a pretty young lady, she was the daughter of the Chief Superintendent. She could park her car anywhere she wanted. One young officer had the cheek to threaten her with a parking offence, but he soon changed his tune when she told him who she was. She was actually stopped by two officers in a police car, for doing fifty-one miles per hour in a built up area. They had the book open to charge her with the offence, but when they learned who she was the book was snapped shut. They drove off after giving her a very timid warning. Kathleen laughed when one of them said, 'Do try to watch your speed, madam.'

Then came the morning she had long tried to obliterate from her memory. Before going to work, she had a message to do for herself in town. She was running a little late, so she parked her car directly under the 'No Parking' sign and walked into the shop to collect her message. It took longer than she had anticipated, so she had to dash, to have any chance of being in time for her work. She sped down the High Street and came onto roadworks that she had forgotten about. They were laying a new sewer, and there was a deep excavation down a long length of the street. There were clear signs, limiting vehicle speeds to twenty miles per hour and forbidding any overtaking.

It was her bad luck to have to follow an old codger through the roadworks. He was keeping to the speed limit: nobody did that. He should not have been out so early, he probably had all day to do what he had to do. Halfway through the road works she overtook him, mistimed an approaching bus, and to avoid the inevitable she swerved into the open excavations. The car finished up wedged tight in the open trench. The doors of the car were so badly damaged that they couldn't be opened, so she was stuck in the car until the firemen came, and they had to call a crane before she could be released from the wreck that had once been her car. She wasn't badly hurt; a broken ankle and a dislocated shoulder were the worst of her injuries.

The inevitable appearance in the Magistrates Court was her biggest nightmare. She sat and listened to the evidence of the old man she had overtaken, the bus driver that she had so nearly hit, and the works foreman who told the Court how his men had had to run in all directions to avoid the out of control car. The men who had been working in the trench had been forced to jump for their lives. Kathleen was given the chance to tell the magistrates her version of how the incident occurred, but it didn't sound good! The magistrates left the Court to deliberate the case. They were only out of the room for a few minutes, but to Kathleen it seemed for ever. Still, after all the evidence she had heard, Kathleen still believed, because of her father's position, that the magistrates would take a lenient view and blame some other factor for the accident.

How wrong she was! The Chief Magistrate removed his glasses and looked at her for quite a while, before saying:

'You are a selfish young lady, whose only thoughts have been for yourself. You have not considered anyone else's safety for one second, and in my opinion you are not responsible enough to wheel a barrow in the street where other people are, let alone be in charge of a potentially lethal motor vehicle.'

At this point the tears began to roll down Kathleen's face, because the magistrate had made her realise how thoughtless and irresponsible she had been.

'I'm going to accept the charge of "Driving without due Care and Attention", for which you will be fined £75, and your licence will be endorsed.'

Kathleen thought that was the end of it, and made to sit down, but the magistrate was not finished.

'Stand still, young lady,' he said, and carried on. 'If anyone else had been hurt besides yourself, you would have been facing the more serious charge of "Dangerous Driving", for which I would have gravely considered sending you to prison. I'm making it quite clear to you now, that if you appear before a court again, for any motoring misdemeanour, this case will be mentioned and the appropriate punishment administered. You may go.'

Kathleen was devastated. She had never been spoken to like that in her life. It frightened her, and the thoughts of it came to her every time she took control of a car. It certainly made her a more considerate, more careful driver.

Despite the bad start, the romance between Kathleen and Frank flourished. They worked for the same firm, and saw a lot of each other. Eventually Frank asked her to marry him, but not without a little cajoling from Kathleen.

Their families organised a party for them, to be held in a conference room in a hotel near Frank's home. Kathleen knew, without asking, that Uncle William and his wife would be invited. The same apprehension came over her, the same disquiet that always came over her when Uncle William was involved. Again her feelings proved to be right. She spoke to Frank, and warned him of the effect Uncle William had on her, and how he could always upset her, how he was 'the fly in the ointment' at every event. Frank however made a joke of it: it didn't affect him in the least.

Both families' friends and relatives were at the occasion, most of them out of the 'top drawer' of society. Frank's mother was in her element, broadcasting the merits of their family to any one who would listen. She made the mistake of telling Uncle William that she was one of the Sin-Clairs of Oakenton. In his piercing voice that could be heard over the whole room, Uncle William said, 'Ah, you must be Peg, old Geordie Sinclair's youngest; ah knew nobody any better. We often used to talk about you, he was proud of you. Him an me had many a good night at the dogs. Mind, that was bad luck he had ower them two piebald Galloways, he should never have got three years over them. Poor fella, he was never the same again.'

Poor Mrs English; if there had been a mousehole handy she would have crawled into it. Kathleen blushed, sharing her embarrassment.

The rest of the evening went well, albeit quietly, for Mrs English was subdued, to say the least. It was another evening Uncle William had ruined for Kathleen. The thought of him sent shudders through her and it tightened the muscles of her face, till she appeared to have a scowl every time she thought of him.

Over the next year arrangements for Kathleen and Frank's marriage progressed steadily. They both held executive positions in their firm. They were well paid, and between them they were comfortably off. They bought a house in Front Street, a fashionable part of town. They spent their time and money having it put to their liking.

Three days before the wedding, Lilian, who was to be Kathleen's chief bridesmaid, arranged to meet Kathleen and Frank to discuss the final arrangements. It was also a chance to have a look around the practically finished house that was to be Kathleen and Frank's home. When she arrived the house had a very wealthy look about it. Kathleen and Frank each had company executive cars sporting consecutive number plates; they looked good, standing in their house driveway. Lilian too was doing very well in her job; she also had a company executive car, but on a slightly higher scale than Kathleen's or Frank's. This needled Kathleen just a little more than it should.

Frank only stayed long enough to show the house off to Lilian, who was duly impressed. He then left to keep an appointment, leaving the two girls to talk. Lilian looked at and admired the wedding dress, then tried on the bridesmaid's dress, which was perfect. They carefully wrapped it in tissue paper, then put it in a stout carrier bag for Lilian to take home, ready for use on the wedding morning.

Kathleen had two tradesmen coming round, one a tiling contractor, the other a painter and decorator. While waiting the two girls sat and talked. The first to call was the tiler. Kathleen, still a bit peeved at Lilian having the better car, embarrassed Lilian with the tirade with which she met the tiler. To Lilian's eyes the work he had done was perfect. Kathleen accused him of putting the picture tiles in the wrong place, and even when the tiler showed her the plan she had given him, she still said he should have known better. She insisted that the offending tiles be moved. Kathleen's next sentence really upset Lilian.

'If you don't make a better job this time my father will hear about it, and you won't get any more work from that quarter.'

All the poor chap could do was grovel, and promise to do the remedial work for nothing. Roughly the same happened with the painter and decorator. She had the whip hand over them, because they both depended, for the most of their work, on the maintenance of police property and a housing charity, all of which depended on the goodwill of the Chief Superintendent, Kathleen's father. Kathleen had taken her peevishness out on them, for Lilian having the better car. The whole episode disturbed Lilian, she really felt for the tradesmen.

After they had left, Kathleen, still on her 'high horse', and not reading Lilian's quickly changing mood, said, 'If only we could think of some way of keeping your Uncle William at home on my wedding day it would make my day for me.'

Lilian flung the bridesmaid's dress on to the stairs. With rage on her face, she said to Kathleen, 'Don't let it worry you, I'll see that none of ours will spoil your day. Find yourself another bridesmaid too.'

Lilian turned on her heel and stormed off. Kathleen, still riding high, locked up and left for home, telling herself it didn't matter, the day would go off better without them.

On the drive over, her balloon burst. The gravity of what she had done began to seep in. By the time she arrived home she was crying her eyes out. 'Damn Uncle William,' she said to herself, 'he can always spoil things.'

When arranging the seating for the wedding reception, Kathleen and her mother had seated Uncle William and his wife to the rear of the room, beside the wall. Her father had looked at the set-up and had placed them right in the middle, among the more preferred guests. No amount of persuasion from Kathleen would change his mind. Luckily her father was out when she walked into the house with the tears streaming down her face. She told her mother what had happened.

Her mother put her arm around her daughter to comfort her, and said, 'Weddings are notorious for causing upsets; come on, love, tidy your face up, we'll go round and see Lilian, and put things right before they get out of hand.'

Lilian hadn't made straight home, and when they arrived only Lilian's mother was at home. Kathleen, the tears starting again, explained what had happened, and that she had to see Lilian, to try and put things right between them. A cup of tea was put in their hands, and Lilian's mother began to talk.

'William can be a bit of a handful, and, as you know, he's a born tease, but his heart's in the right place. Our Lilian thinks the world of him, and she appreciates his efforts in running the shop.'

Kathleen butted in. 'But you and your sister, his wife, run the shop.'

'No, dear, my sister and I couldn't run a Sunday School picnic between us. Oh, it's his way to take a back seat, but it's he who does it all. Years ago my sister was all set to marry a chap but he jilted her. For months she wouldn't leave the house. We thought her breakdown was going to be permanent. William came on the scene, and was wonderful to her. He gradually helped her to regain her confidence by giving her a responsible position in the shop. He eventually married her; he undoubtedly saved her sanity. He did, off and on, the same for me. Jack, my husband, walked out on Lilian and me when she was just a baby, but William gave me a job in the shop, which helped me back on my feet, and William has been a better father to Lilian than Jack could ever have been. William paid for Lilian's education too, and she adores him for it. She knows it gave her a chance in life that she would never have had. He was good to your father too, but to his credit Young Stan has never forgotten him. Young Stan's father, your grandfather, he's long dead now, poor chap. He never enjoyed good health, and lost a lot of work through sickness, no fault of his own, but his family would have gone to bed hungry on many occasions if it hadn't been for William, and he did the same for a lot of others. Another thing he did for Young Stan: when he applied to join the police, his education and fitness were not quite up to their standards, and they turned him down. William knew some of the members of the Watch Committee. He swayed them to reconsider your father's application, and he was taken on. Mind, he's done wonderfully well, through his hard work, but it was William who got him the chance. As I said before, Young Stan has never forgotten him, and I think he would be upset if William didn't attend your wedding. For the life of me, I can't see our Lilian doing anything to upset the apple cart.'

At this point Lilian returned home. Kathleen walked over to her, her face still tear-stained. Her apologies to Lilian were genuine. She pleaded with her to forget what had been said, and, 'Would you please still be my bridesmaid?'

Lilian put her arms around her, to pacify her, and assured her that she would be happy to be her bridesmaid. Then, with baited breath Kathleen said, 'Have you said anything to your Uncle William?'

As predicted by her mother, Lilian had far more sense than to do anything like that. Kathleen, always the emotional one, threw her arms round Lilian and burst into tears again.

The wedding day was beautiful, fine, sunny and warm. The church service was perfect. Perhaps things were going off too well, maybe the atmosphere a little too 'stuffed shirt'. It was all change at the reception, which was held in an hotel. The guests were served with sherry and waited in the lobby till the bride and groom were ready to receive them in the ballroom. There were four waiters and six waitresses, lined up neatly beside the wall waiting to serve the guests.

One of Frank's aunts said in a supercilious tone, 'One can hardly tell the difference between the waiters and the guests.'

Uncle William heard her, and answered in his piercing voice, 'Oh, no, Missus, it's easy; the waiters have clean shirts.'

There were a few red faces and a few grins at Uncle William's observations. It had the effect of loosening up the spirit of the event. But what really livened up the proceedings was what happened as the bride and groom welcomed their guests to the reception. Kathleen and her husband Frank stood in front of the stage in the hotel ballroom. The stage would have been for the band, if it had been a ball. The guests filed slowly past, congratulated them, and, as was tradition, kissed the bride. It came to Uncle William to congratulate them. He shook Frank's hand, pecked Kathleen on the cheek and, holding her hand, said to her, 'By gum, lassie, yer looking luvly t'day. By, if ah'd been a year or two younger, by ah'd given that young whippersnapper a run for his money.'

Kathleen had been a very active member of Miss Snowball's drama class at East Oakenton High School for Girls. She had on many occasions taken a principal role in the Shakespearean plays that had been performed. With one backward step, she was on the ballroom stage. She played the role of her life, and paid back Uncle William for all the teasing that she had endured over the years. With arms outstretched toward him, and with all the right expressions on her face, she began, 'Good Sire, hadst thou to wait till this too late hour to make thine feelings towards me clear.'

Most of the wedding party knew how Uncle William had tormented her over the years. They all laughed and enjoyed the impromptu performance. Uncle William tried to escape to his seat, but Mrs Makepeace was behind him. She made him stand and endure the 'turned tables'.

'Thee says thou art in thine Autumn days. To me hast thou not been forever in thy Springtime? Surely thy eternal Summers shall not fade! Thou couldst have promised me such a beauteous day, instead thou chose to wet a maiden's eye. Ye have allowed thy swiftfooted time glass make me forever absent from thine heart. How heavy will I journey on my way, for methinks no face as gracious as thine.'

Kathleen lowered her face and curtseyed gracefully. The whole wedding party, including Frank, applauded, and poor Uncle William, face red, was allowed to shuffle to his seat, muttering something about 'the daft young blighters'.

The incident eased the wedding reception into a lighthearted atmosphere. The meal was enjoyed in a relaxed climate, and the wedding celebrated, as it should be, in a cheerful manner.

Two years after the wedding, William Makepeace had a heart attack and died. Half the town attended his funeral. There were so many mourners they couldn't be accommodated in the church. Dozens had to listen to the service via a hastily arranged loudspeaker positioned at the church door. William's wife, who was well past retiring age, sold the business and moved in with her sister. It was a good move. Having worked together over the years they knew each other's moods intimately, and Lilian no longer lived at home. She had her own flat, and promotion at work meant she travelled all over the world.

Charlie, still gazing at the shop, said out loud, 'Old William was certainly a character.'

Two women, walking by, heard him and gave him a disdainful look. It was sad. Several others tried to keep the business going under William's name, but none lasted more than a month or two: the competition was too hard. It depressed Charlie to see the shop derelict.

CHAPTER 14

Without moving his feet, Charlie's gaze shifted to the shop directly next door. It was an electrical shop that sold and rented televisions, radios and the like. It was a bright shop, with lots of lights in the window and always two or three televisions working. Charlie had never owned a television, and had no desire to. Fred Harding had been very keen on them, and had been one of the first to own one. Charlie had had many invitations to have an evening's viewing, but it was something he had always declined. He was much happier spending the evening in the White Swan, but he never refused Fred's invitation to watch the FA Cup Final every year. It was a real treat for Charlie, who had always enjoyed a good football match. Because of being so nearly killed at the last live match he attended, in all the years he had not been able to join another crowd in a stadium. Charlie would buy a few bottles of beer and Fred's wife would make a plateful of sandwiches. At half past two on the May Saturday afternoon, the set was turned on, and they watched the show-piece match and enjoyed the entertainment. Charlie pondered a while, and thought to himself, 'I'm not going to buy a television, and pay the licence, just so as I can watch the Cup Final.' Then an idea came to him. He remembered that the White Swan had a set in the new lounge bar. He made up his mind: 'I'll watch it in there.'

Still looking at the electrical shop, he remembered he had been a customer there. Just before last Christmas, his radio had broken down, and he and Fred had taken it to the shop, to see if it could be repaired. The girl in the shop had said to them, 'Don't be daft, lads, it's going to cost more to repair than you could have a new one for.' Charlie had hesitated, but the girl was a good saleswoman; in the end she had convinced him. He bought a new radio, and became a customer. Coming out of the shop, they had looked at the televisions in the window. Fred, in his philosophical mood, had said, 'Charlie, you know, they pay some of these singers on the television thousands and thousands of pounds, but in my opinion they're not half as good as Bertie Howard's grand-daughter, when she gives us a song in the White Swan.' Bertie Howard's grand-daughter usually came into the White Swan on a holiday week-end, and sang to the patrons. 'Easter Bonnet', and 'Old Shep' were Charlie's favourites.

A solemn smile came on Charlie's lips, as he remembered Fred again. 'Aye, you were right there, Fred, me old matey.'

CHAPTER 15

A ll the speculation on the likelihood of war was suddenly over. What everyone had dreaded had arrived. War was declared. It was the biggest upset in Charlie's life, and in everyone else's lives. Charlie's age group was one of the first to have to register for Army service. All plans for marriage had to be shelved, but he and Lilly did have an understanding. As soon as things settled down again, they would marry, and move into their house. In the meantime the house would have to be let to help pay off the loan. Things moved quickly, and soon after registering, he and several other young men from the foundry were told to report for a medical. It was here that Charlie learned that his spell behind the plough on Alex Brass's farm had permanently damaged his feet. It was a blow to Charlie; it made him unfit for most of the Army Units, such as Infantry and Artillery Regiments, which were the ones he had expected to join.

Weeks went by, and Charlie heard nothing from the authorities. The other young chaps at the foundry, with whom he had registered, had all had their call-up papers and were assigned to their various regiments. Charlie was beginning to feel guilty, and was starting to think that he was unwanted in the Armed Services. It was almost a relief when his call-up papers did come, and he was surprised to find that he was to be taken into the RAF. He was to report to their training camp in seven days.

The camp was local, and easily reached by the local bus service. There were another fourteen young fellows in Charlie's intake. They were allocated two wooden huts, which were equipped with the bare minimum of amenities, just a metal bed and a metal wardrobe each. Sergeant Flowers was in charge of them. Charlie took an immediate dislike to him. He abused the power he had, by intimidating his charges. He was sadistic and a bully.

One of Charlie's fellow recruits, Billy Armstrong, was a twenty-year-old but he looked no older than about fourteen. He had travelled in on the same bus as Charlie, and was so young looking that the conductor had only charged him half fare. He was so small that the stores had trouble kitting him out; his uniform and boots were obviously a size too big. The lad did his best with the exercises and marches that were part of the training, but they were too much for him; it was easy to see that he wasn't strong enough to take it. Charlie and the rest of the lads were sorry for him and did their best to help. Every evening he was exhausted, and his feet were in a terrible state, as the boots had given him blisters. Yet he was surprisingly tough and resilient. There was nothing wrong with his will or determination. It was his physique that let him down, and never a word of complaint passed his lips. Sergeant Flowers bawled at him continually and showed him up by using his physical incapability as an example to the rest of the squad.

About nine o'clock one morning, fourteen days into their training, they had already had a session of physical exercises, to 'warm them up', as the Sergeant said, for the route march that was to follow. Someone from the Administration Hut pushed a note into Sergeant Flower's hand. He read it and bawled at Billy, 'Armstrong, fall out, get out of that uniform and into your civvies, hand your uniform back into the Stores, report to the Officer in Administration, and look slippy about it.'

While Billy was still in earshot, he said to the rest of the squad, 'I always said the little worm wouldn't make it; perhaps now we'll get some serious training in.'

Everyone thought that Billy was being rejected because of his physical drawbacks, and didn't expect to see him again. Two hours later, when they returned from the route march, they were amazed to find Billy sitting on his bed, his face lit up in a smile.

'What's all this, then?' bawled the Sergeant.

'I'm being transferred to another branch of the Service, Sir.'

'Which other branch?'

'Not allowed to say, Sir.'

Sergeant Flowers was speechless, and strode out of the hut. Billy had stayed to say good-bye to his mates in the hut, and he confided in them and told them what had happened. His father had been a lecturer in Germany for many years, and a lot of Billy's education had been in Germany. He spoke the language perfectly, and knew a lot of the country's culture.

'I'm going into Intelligence,' he said quietly. 'I'm to work in civvies, and I'm being transferred to London.'

All his mates from the hut walked with him to the staff car that was waiting to take him to the railway station. He was waving like royalty, as he was driven away.

Charlie had always been used to having a purpose in all that he did, but he couldn't see any sense in the regimentation, physical exercises, and marching aimlessly all over the countryside. Being taken on a ten-mile route march, starting and finishing on the same spot, seemed to be the ultimate in stupidity. All this was compounded by being torn away from Lilly and denied the beer that had been his lifeblood at the foundry. The last straw was Sergeant Flowers' constant bawling and intimidation. At seven o'clock one wet morning, Charlie's temper snapped. He told the Sergeant exactly what he thought of him and refused to turn out for the drill session. The Sergeant turned bright red in the face with anger. Charlie thought he was going to burst, he was so puffed up with rage. Charlie held his ground and refused to budge. In the end all the Sergeant could do was confine him to the hut and threaten to take him to the Commanding Officer.

About ten o'clock that morning, Charlie was marched in to see Group Captain Hedley, the Officer in Charge. Sergeant Flowers barked out the charges Charlie was to answer to.

'Has Hammond been difficult in any other way?' The Group Captain asked.

'No, Sir,' was the prompt reply.

'Then leave us, Sergeant, please.'

'Yes, Sir.'

'Sit down, Hammond,' he said to Charlie. Charlie sat down, and had a good look at the Group Captain, who had a kindly face. It was quite obvious that in normal times, he would have been retired.

'Now then, son,' he said, 'What's all this about?'

'Can't see any sense in it, Sir, jumping up and down in the teeming rain, like someone not right in the head.'

The Group Captain smiled. 'You are not from a military family, are you, son?'

Charlie's dander was still up. 'I beg your pardon, Sir, but my father was gassed in the last war, it killed him in the end.'

'I'm sorry about that, lad, but that's not what I meant. I'm talking about families that live for nothing other than His Majesty's Service.'

'I see what you mean, Sir.'

'I know it's difficult for you to understand Service life, when you have only ever experienced commercial life. The training you are doing is important. It's difficult to picture the RAF as soldiers, but primarily, that's what we are. It does not matter whether we are a Squadron Leader or a sweeper-up, if it comes to the crunch we have to stand shoulder to shoulder with our contemporaries and fight our enemies. I can see you are not an awkward young fellow, and I think you're going to tell me that this incident is just a "flash in the pan"; am I right in thinking this?'

'Yes, Sir.'

'You realise I have to punish you?'

'Yes, Sir.'

'Then you are confined to barracks for three days. I won't spoil your forty-eight hour weekend leave. Is that clear to you?'

'Yes, Sir.'

'Then dismiss, and rejoin your squad.'

It was the first time Charlie had been spoken to with any degree of civility since he had been called up. It went a long way in helping him settle to RAF life.

After his forty-eight hour leave, the training changed to much fewer physical exercises, as weapon training came to the forefront. Sergeant Flower's sadistic streak came out again. John Tucker, a most unlikeable member of the squad, obviously had had some poaching experience, for he mastered the rifle quite well. He was held up as an example to the rest of the squad by Sergeant Flowers. It was the most humiliating action he could possibly have taken. The fellow snored like a trooper, making it difficult for the rest of the squad to sleep, there was a constant pungent smell from him, his speech was slurred, like a drunken man, and his table manners were atrocious. Charlie didn't have a delicate stomach, but sitting at the table with John Tucker, watching him, head down, shovelling porridge into his mouth, put Charlie and many others off their food. One lad hit the nail on the head when he said, 'He's not quite all there.'

It was the squad's first practice with a rifle; they had been given instruction with it, but this was the first time they were actually to fire the weapon. John Tucker was chosen by Sergeant Flowers to demonstrate to the others what to do. John was beaming all over his face, as he confidently fitted his clip of bullets to the rifle. His five bullets all hit the wooden cut-out of a German soldier.

'That's the way I want to see you all shooting,' the Sergeant said with a smirk. 'Now, let's see the rest of you layabouts approach me one at a time and do half as well as Tucker here.'

It came to Charlie's turn, and, like most of the others in the squad, he was hopeless with the rifle which was only to be expected as the only gun he had ever had in his hand was an air rifle at a fairground. The bolt on the rifle needed a good positive action to remove the spent cartridge and put a live one into the breech. He was so nervous, and so afraid of the rifle, that his actions were weak and half-hearted. It jammed with every bullet, incurring the wrath of Sergeant Flowers who had to free the rifle for him before every shot, but Charlie did manage to hit the target with three of his attempts. After a while, with much shouting and badgering from the Sergeant, Charlie and the rest of the squad became reasonably proficient with the Enfield rifle. Sergeant Flowers had to rile the squad by bawling, 'You useless lot, you'll never be as good as Tucker.'

The next part of the training was how to use a hand-grenade. Because everyone knew that the practice grenade was a harmless dummy, no one was nervous, and the routine was soon mastered.

Charlie would never forget the next stage of their training. It was with the hand-held machine gun, so widely used by the Army. As Sergeant Flowers pointed out, they were in such short supply, they were lucky to have one to practise with. He spent a whole day explaining the workings of the machine gun. The following day they were each to fire a small burst at the target. Sand-bags were arranged in a crescent shape, and the machine gun and the magazine were lying separately on top of them. Sergeant Flowers explained that they were each to pick up the weapon, fit the magazine, fire a short burst at the target, remove the magazine, and replace it on the sand bags. The whole squad were terrified. As expected, John Tucker was invited up first to demonstrate. He nonchalantly picked up the weapon, slammed the magazine into it, fired at the target, and turned to accept his accolades. But the useless great stupid oaf still had the trigger squeezed. Bullets were spraying everywhere. Luckily he had lowered the gun; the bullets were hitting the ground a few yards in front of him. There were lumps of concrete and tarmac flying everywhere, as the bullets tore into the ground.

Sergeant Flowers was in the forefront, and was hit in the right leg. He was a strong man and didn't go down; if he had he'd surely have been killed. Someone shouted, 'Run!' Charlie and the rest of the squad were about three steps in front of that command. Sergeant Smith, who was in charge of a similar squad, saw what was happening from fifty yards away. He ran towards John Tucker. The gun ran out of ammunition before he had made ten yards, but he kept running at him. The incident was over, yet he still leapt at him and bore him to the ground, as in a hard rugby tackle. John Tucker was in a state of bewilderment, besides being groggy from being knocked to the ground. Sergeant Smith ordered two of his men to escort Tucker inside and to keep guard over him.

Sergeant Flowers was the only one seriously hurt. Of the Squad, one had a gash on his ear, caused by a piece of flying concrete, another had the heel of his boot shot off. It was John Tucker's last day in the RAF; he was removed as 'unsuitable material'. The rest of their training was carried out under Sergeant Smith, thankfully without any more incidents.

Charlie was given seven days' leave, and was told to expect notice, in that time, as to where he would be posted. Three days later he had a letter, with instructions to report to Beaconbroad, which was an airfield near a village of that name in Norfolk. Included was a travel warrant and a letter to present on his arrival. He spent every evening of his leave with Lilly, and in that time he felt closer to her than he ever had. It would be an understatement to say he was sorry when his leave was up and he had to take the train to his posting.

It was a gruelling train journey that took all of ten hours. Thankfully there was an RAF truck to meet the train, for the airfield was five miles or more from the station. On arrival he handed his letter to Administration, and was shown to the hut where he was to be billeted. He was to share with three others, and the facilities were sparse, much the same as they had been at the training camp: a metal single bed and a metal locker each. He was told to report to Sergeant Atkinson, in the maintenance hangar, as soon as his belongings were stowed.

'Are you a driver?' was the first question Sergeant Atkinson asked him.

'No, Sir,' answered Charlie.

'It's a driver I asked for; have you had any driving experience at all?'

Charlie explained how he had worked at the foundry where they had a Chaseside loading shovel that was used for moving the scrap iron. He had spent odd days driving that machine, and a neighbour had an old motor bike which he had ridden down the back streets on occasions. It had been so unreliable that they had spent more time pushing it than riding it.

'First thing in the morning I want you to report to Sergeant Murphy, he's in charge of transport. Tell him I sent you, and ask him if there's any chance of him making you a driver.'

'Yes, Sir,' answered Charlie.

Charlie duly reported to Sergeant Murphy, a massive Irishman who, Charlie decided, in different times would have been quite at home supervising a team of road builders, pipelayers, or something similar. Charlie thought he was going to be given some sort of instruction in driving. Instead the Sergeant pointed to the fifteen hundredweight, covered-in truck that had met the train the previous day. In his broad Irish twang, he said, 'Let's see how you manage, then. I want you to drive the truck between those two jerry cans on the left, pull it hard round, then through those other two on the right. Take it right round the perimeter, pull back in here, and stand it where it stands now. Have you got that?'

'Yes, Sir.'

Charlie climbed into the driving seat. Sergeant Murphy took the passenger seat.

'OK, get on with it, we haven't got all day.'

Charlie turned on the ignition toggle switch and pressed the starter. The vehicle was still in gear, so it leapt forward a couple of yards and stopped with a jolt, banging the Sergeant's head off the windscreen in the process. Undeterred Charlie moved the gear lever to neutral and started again. The engine fired and ran smoothly; he depressed the clutch pedal, selected first gear, lightly eased the accelerator to speed up the engine, and took his foot off the clutch pedal. The truck shot forward, throwing his weight off the accelerator, which had the effect of slowing the vehicle violently. In correcting the fault, he put too much pressure on the accelerator, and the truck leapt forward again. The process was repeated, and progress was made with a series of terrifying kangaroo leaps. The Sergeant caught his leg on a clip that held the engine cover down. It tore an 'L'-shaped piece from his uniform, and gashed his leg. In all this, Charlie was frantically wrestling with the steering wheel, trying to steer between the jerry cans. He hadn't a chance. He ran straight over the first one, which exploded like a burst tyre. The second one he just touched with the front wheel. It shot over the ground, like an orange pip squeezed between finger and thumb.

Out on the perimeter track, it wasn't so bad; he was able to engage a higher gear and the truck ran relatively smoothly, but all too soon he was back to the compound, and his troubles started again. The gears rasped as he tried to re-engage the lower gears; he had underestimated his speed, and had to stamp on the brake. It had been a hair raising ride. When he eventually switched off the engine, he was thirty yards from where he should have parked the truck. Charlie then had to face Sergeant Murphy, who was red faced with rage, a bruise on his forehead where he had hit the windscreen and blood trickling down his torn uniform trousers.

Charlie had been surrounded by men all his life, in the back streets, at the farm, in the foundry, and in the RAF. He thought he had heard some good swearers, but none could come anywhere near Sergeant Murphy. He was swearing for a long time before Charlie could understand anything he was saying. Gradually, through the haze of swearing, Charlie got the gist of what was being said. According to the Sergeant, if Charlie had really wanted to help the war effort, he would have done more good joining the German Army. Still, however, through the obscurity of swearing, Charlie realised that the Sergeant was going to sign the necessary papers to allow him to drive RAF vehicles. Then the Sergeant laid down his own conditions. Charlie could drive with the proviso he didn't go within fifty yards of any personnel, buildings, fixtures, or, most of all, an aircraft, until he was proficient. If he caused the Sergeant any trouble, or got him in hot water in any way, he would personally castrate him, and kick the removed articles the full length of the runway, one at a time.

Charlie reported to Sergeant Atkinson. 'Well,' he said. 'Sergeant Murphy said I could drive for you, but only if I don't go near any installation or machine till I've had some practice.'

There was a vehicle similar to the one that Charlie had so disastrously driven, standing by the hangar. Sergeant Atkinson nodded towards it, and told Charlie to take it to a quiet place, at the far end of the airfield, and familiarise himself with it. Charlie managed much better on his own, and very soon mastered the controls of the vehicle. After half an hour out of sight of anyone, he was able to start, change gear and stop, smoothly and confidently.

From then on he felt part of things. He was something, he was a driver in the RAF, working under Sergeant Atkinson. He was a bit of a 'dogsbody' really. Sergeant Atkinson was in charge of the maintenance hangar, with six hard-worked engineers under him. Beaconbroad was the home of a Fighter Squadron. The Sergeant was responsible for the maintenance of their planes. There were usually twelve to fifteen fighters on the base. Charlie was at the beck and call of the engineers, and soon knew them well. He fetched and carried for them, he lugged spare parts into and out of the stores, he drove the small tractor and pulled fighter planes into and out of the maintenance hanger, always with two engineers guiding the tail of the aircraft to make sure it followed in a straight line. He swept up after them, and was often asked to sit in the cockpit and operate various controls while the engineers made adjustments. In the process he learned quite a lot about the fighters, even the starting procedure. He did errands in the fifteen-hundredweight truck, and soon knew the roads in the area like the back of his hand. He was often called on to collect and deliver spares to and from other Squadrons, and he was a regular visitor to the railway station, collecting parcels and taxiing personnel to and fro. Being so busy, with so much going on, and being part of it, made time go very quickly.

Because of severe staff shortage, Sergeant Atkinson was in temporary charge of fuel deliveries for the Squadron. One morning, just after eight o'clock, Charlie had only been on duty for about half an hour when two massive road tankers full of aviation fuel pulled up in front of the hangar. Everyone stared in disbelief when the drivers climbed down from their cabs. They were two girls, no more than about five feet tall, who could have been twins. They had identical features, hair-styles, and overalls.

Sergeant Atkinson spoke to Charlie: 'Heaven help us, lad, look what we have here; they look to me to be more dangerous than Hitler. Such tender young ladies, to be in charge of such lethal cargo. Go with them to the fuel dump and watch them like a hawk; they could just as easily blow us into the middle of next week.'

The Sergeant needn't have worried for they were two very capable young girls. Charlie had had some experience with fuel deliveries. If the lorries were positioned just right, two could be off-loaded together. He stood on the running board of the first lorry, guided it into position, and indicated to the other where she was to stand. Simultaneously they were off-loaded, everything done according to the rules. The procedure passed quickly and safely. Charlie enjoyed the company of the girls, escorted them to have their papers signed and walked with them to their lorries. Charlie said his goodbyes and was walking away when one of the girls called to him.

'Just a minute, Charlie, let's see if we have anything for you.'

One of them climbed up into the cab and passed down a box of eating apples and a box of chocolate bars, the type that were used in vending machines.

'Where on earth have you got these?' Charlie said with his mouth open.

'It's amazing what goes astray in the docks these days,' she said, touching her nose.

Charlie was struggling to hold the two heavy boxes. One of the girls pecked him on the cheek, then, smiling, they said in unison, 'See you again, Charlie,' and they were on their way. Charlie lugged the boxes into the hangar, and put them on the Sergeant's bench. News soon travelled round the base, and everyone found an excuse to call at the hangar. Each was given an apple and a bar of chocolate; they were a real luxury. Charlie was flavour of the month.

The engineers were expecting delivery of a new Spitfire. It was to be delivered by Anne, a popular girl who had been a regular visitor to the squadron over the last eighteen months. She was a member of the special corps of pilots who specialised in the delivery of aeroplanes to the

RAF. She was sighted when she circled the airfield prior to landing. Charlie was with two of the engineers who had come out of the hanger to watch her land. The Spitfire was approaching normally, wheels down, when suddenly, with the plane only about sixty feet from the ground, the left hand wing dipped alarmingly. The engine roared as Anne snapped the throttle open. The Spitfire travelled the length of the field, the wing tip only feet from the ground. Painfully slowly the plane levelled out as it gained speed. While the plane circled the field, there was speculation as to the problem with the Spitfire. There were various observations as to its troubles, but the common denominator was a fault with one of the control surfaces. Something had either broken or come out of adjustment, after the plane had left the factory.

The engineers were unanimous in deciding there was no way Anne was going to land the Spitfire. She should head it out to sea and bail out. The Spitfire, being new, was not fully fitted out; it was yet to be fitted with wireless. Anne was on her own, she couldn't take any advice. After circling for about twenty minutes, the Spitfire banked away, and seconds later it hurtled the length of the field, head height, at tremendous speed. It was the most frightening experience of Charlie's life. A few minutes later, Anne repeated the exercise, and one of the engineers said, 'She's going to try and land, at that speed.'

A few minutes later, sure enough, she approached the runway again, still doing the same speed, this time with wheels down. The plane must have been doing three times the normal landing speed. It was a brilliant piece of flying, but the first touch of the wheels, right opposite where Charlie was standing, brought smoke pouring from them. The Spitfire leapt and lurched in a frightening manner. Charlie thought it was going to disintegrate, but Anne controlled it. She took the full length of the field to bring it to rest, but the Spitfire was on the ground, and in one piece. Everyone who had watched her dashed over to congratulate her and show appreciation for the skill she had shown in bringing the faulty Spitfire safely to the ground.

Charlie took stock one night, while lying in bed. He was surprised, when he worked it out, that he had been in the RAF for over two years. The war was on a knife edge. The pilots were so hard pressed, they barely had time to sleep, they were so often called on to fight off enemy bombers and to escort our own bombers home. With heartbreaking regularity some didn't return. All the ground staff knew the pressure and strain the pilots were under and all did their best, in whatever were their duties, to ease the pilots' burdens.

One of the pilots was very difficult to help; he held too high an opinion of himself. He had come into the RAF straight from university, and thought himself a cut above everyone else. Elders was his name. The pilots were regular visitors to the maintenance hangar and the engineers listened carefully, when they described any faults in their planes. Elders however treated them like imbeciles, and he referred to the fighter planes as 'kites', something Sergeant Atkinson couldn't stand. To the maintenance crew, Elders was bad news, and very much disliked. Even Charlie had a run in with him. After maintenance work it was imperative that the cockpits were scrupulously clean. Charlie was often called on to do it, and he made such a good job of it that Sergeant Atkinson no longer examined the finished work. Charlie was cleaning the cockpit of a Spitfire after some major work had been done on it. He knew only too well the dangers of dust and debris floating about when the plane was in flight. Halfway through his cleaning job, Elders came on the scene. He dressed Charlie down, ranted about how important it was to have the cockpit clean, and questioned Charlie's ability to do the work. If it had been civilian life, Charlie would have thrown the brush and cleaning materials at him and would have told him to do it himself. As it was, he had to swallow his pride, say 'Yes, Sir,' and carry on with his work.

Sergeant Atkinson and two of the engineers also had a 'run in' with him, this time over the performance of his Spitfire. Elders claimed he had been forced to leave the Squadron, leaving them a plane short, when the Squadron were in a dangerous position. He had complained of fluctuating oil pressure in the Spitfire engine. He had raged at Sergeant Atkinson and the two engineers, after they had spent all day going through the engine with a fine-tooth comb and had been unable to find any fault. In the early hours of one Friday morning, before Charlie came on duty, he heard the Squadron take off, at about 5.00 a.m. An hour later Charlie was in the maintenance hangar, along with Sergeant Atkinson and three of the engineers. They heard a lone Spitfire land. It taxied right up to the hangar opening. Elders climbed down from the plane. He was furious and screamed at Sergeant Atkinson, complaining that after three quarters of an hour, the engine of his Spitfire was spluttering and losing power. He hurled abuse at the Sergeant and the engineers, telling them they weren't fit to maintain his sister's push-bike. He wanted the engine stripped and the fault found now.

Out of the corner of his eye, Charlie caught sight of Group Captain Willis, the Station Commander, coming into the hangar with an armed guard marching at his side. Charlie nudged the Sergeant to draw his attention to them.

'Attention!' shouted Sergeant Atkinson, and everyone dropped what they were doing.

Without breaking stride, the Station Commander barked back, 'Carry on as you were.' He ignored Elders, and spoke only to the Sergeant. 'Has that machine been touched since it came in?'

'No, Sir.'

'Good. I don't want it touched till I give my personal permission, you understand that, Sergeant?'

'Yes, Sir.'

He nodded toward the guard. 'I'm leaving this guard to make sure this machine is not touched until I'm ready. You do understand what I'm saying, Sergeant?'

'Yes, Sir.'

Without another word, the guard took up station by the Spitfire and the Station Commander left the hangar, followed after a few minutes by Elders.

Half an hour later, the rest of the Squadron returned. Ten minutes after that, the Station Commander returned to the hangar, this time accompanied by Squadron Leader Walker. The Station Commander asked Sergeant Atkinson, 'Can you spare us anyone to help us test this Spitfire?'

All the engineers were overwhelmed with work, as on top of all the usual maintenance work, one of the planes had landed heavily on one of its wheels. It would take two of the engineers all day to repair and test the machine. The Sergeant nodded towards Charlie, who was busy unpacking spares. 'Would Hammond do, Sir?'

'Yes, he'll do fine.'

Charlie was called over to join the group. 'Hammond, you're to help in a test on the Spitfire,' the Sergeant told him.

Squadron Leader Walker gave Charlie his instructions. 'Bring your tow-tractor, and pull the Spitfire onto the grass, well away from the hangar. Ask the bowser driver to put fuel in it, enough for two hours, then chock the plane firmly.'

Charlie hurried about his duties, and felt about ten feet tall, towing the Spitfire with the Station Commander and Squadron Leader Walker guiding its tail. While the bowser driver fuelled the plane, Charlie brought the special chocks, with the fifteen-hundredweight truck that they always used in an engine test. Then came instructions from Squadron Leader Walker that took Charlie's breath away.

'I want you to start her up and sit with her for about three quarters of an hour. Keep varying the throttle setting, so that the engine is revving between about a thousand to fourteen hundred revs. If there is any sign of anything wrong, switch off immediately and report to me. I'll be back in about three quarters of an hour. Is that clear?'

'Yes, Sir.' Charlie's knees had turned to jelly with nerves, as he climbed into the cockpit. Thankfully he knew what was expected of him, and went through the starting procedure perfectly. The engine roared into life the moment he pressed the start button. It was the most wondrous hour of his life, feeling the vibrations of the powerful engine right through his body, as he gently altered the throttle setting. He was very much aware that the Spitfire was still fully armed. It was a 'top of the world' feeling, looking through the gun sights, and holding the controls.

The three quarters of an hour was over too soon and the Squadron Leader was back. The plane engine was too noisy to hold a conversation, but by a series of signs Charlie indicated everything was OK. They exchanged places and, at a signal from the Squadron Leader, Charlie removed the chocks. Two minutes after that the Spitfire was airborne. Charlie and the guard stood by the fifteen-hundredweight truck and watched as the Squadron Leader put the Spitfire through its paces. It was a terrific display of flying. The plane hardly left the confines of the airfield, but the Squadron Leader put it through every manoeuvre in the book. He dived to within feet of the ground, climbed till the plane stalled and, with masterful flying, recovered control when he seemed sure to crash. He rolled and looped several times and finally, before landing, flew the length of the field, feet from the ground, upside down.

111

The Squadron Leader walked over to where Charlie and the guard were standing. 'It's Charlie, isn't it?'

'Yes, Sir.'

Grinning like a Cheshire cat, the Squadron Leader said, 'Charlie, if it had been a two-seater I'd have taken you up with me!'

'Thank you, Sir, that was a very kind thought, I'd have appreciated that,' Charlie answered with an equally big grin.

Elders was not seen on the base again. It was reckoned the conclusion wasn't too hard to fathom.

The tide of the war was turning, and the mood throughout the base was lightening. After the incident with Elders' Spitfire, Charlie was held in a little more esteem in the maintenance hangar. This in turn boosted his confidence; he was really enjoying his work with the Spitfires.

A few months later, the American base that was about twenty miles from Beaconbroad were expecting delivery of twenty Flying Fortress bombers. They were being flown directly from America. About an hour before they were due to land, the American base was bombed and there was panic in finding alternative landing sites for them. Four of the Flying Fortresses were diverted to Beaconbroad. They landed safely, but the big problem was that the airfield wasn't big enough for them to take off again, or not with any degree of safety. Charlie was called upon to tow the gigantic bombers to the perimeter fence at the far side of the airfield. Car-loads of American servicemen arrived, who set up camp around the newly arrived bombers. It was a sort of camp within a camp.

The American guards were very keen, and wouldn't allow British personnel near their bombers. Except Charlie. The Americans had asked for the use of a truck and driver to fetch and carry for them, and Charlie had been nominated. The day after their arrival, Charlie had made one run to the American base for mechanical spares, and was then asked to return in the afternoon for foodstuffs. It was difficult to obtain entry to the American Base, he had to pass two check points and know the pass-word, but once inside, security wasn't too tight. When he saw inside their foodstore, his eyes opened wide: it was bursting at the seams with foodstuffs the like of which Charlie hadn't seen for years. He couldn't resist it: when the order was complete he calmly added a case of tinned steak and a case of tinned fruit to the order. Halfway back to the Base he stopped, and hid the two cases under a sheet. After delivering the American's order, he felt a little guilty. He showed Sergeant Atkinson what he had done, and asked his advice on what to do with his ill gotten gains.

'Take it straight round to our cook, he'll treasure you for ever.'

The Sergeant was right; the Corporal in charge of the cooking was ecstatic when given the two cases.

'Will they not miss it, Charlie?'

'I wish you could see inside their stores, they are laden with this sort of stuff.'

'Well then, we'll all eat well for a day or two, and if you get the chance, bring as much of this sort of stuff as you can fiddle.'

'Yes, I will.'

It took another two weeks to lengthen the runway and gather together four top Flying Fortress pilots with the ability to take off from Beaconbroad. In the meantime, Charlie was called upon to do numerous trips to the American stores. It was so easy, he was soon bringing as much food, under the tarpaulin sheet, to the British side, as he was to the Americans.

When the big day finally came for the giant bombers to leave, Charlie was called upon to tow the aeroplanes to the dispersal point. They were carrying the minimum amount of fuel and only two crew, to keep the weight down as much as possible. Charlie towed the first one, and by the time he had the second one on tow, the first one had two of its engines started. Charlie was able to sit on the tractor and watch as the other two were started. It taxied to the runway end and stood awhile till the engines warmed. Then there was an ear-shattering roar as the pilot opened the throttles. It gained speed pitifully slowly; Charlie thought it would never make flying speed in the available space but, with just a few yards left, the giant plane left the ground, black smoke pouring from its exhausts. The first one was up and away. It was a carbon copy with the other three. Everyone on the base had turned out to watch, and there were cheers as each of the bombers took to the air.

The Americans were elated to see the operation go so smoothly, and within the hour they were packed up and moving back to their own Base. The last to leave was Major Rawlings, who had been in charge of the American contingent. He had his driver drop him at the maintenance hangar; he walked in and asked Sergeant Atkinson if he could speak to Charlie. Charlie saluted respectfully.

'Ah wanna thank you, Charlie boy,' the Major said in his strong Southern accent. 'You've looked after us real well, will you accept this small present as a thank you.' He handed Charlie a cardboard box; there was a bottle of Bourbon, and a carton of two hundred Camel cigarettes in it.

Charlie felt dreadful, he had robbed them rotten for nearly three weeks, and their Top Brass had come personally, brought him a present, and thanked him for what he had done. Charlie didn't smoke, so he gave the cigarettes to the engineers in the hangar. He and another four or five usually had a game of cards on a Sunday night. Charlie put the bottle of Bourbon on the table and they toasted the Americans three or four times.

The incident with the Americans was the last highlight in Charlie's RAF career. The war was going all the Allies' way. The work in the maintenance hangar was down to a fine art, everyone was on top of their jobs. It gave Charlie a lot of satisfaction, working with the engineers and the aeroplanes. He loved his driving, especially when he was able to leave the base, and drive on the local roads. Then suddenly it was all over; the war in Europe was won. There were celebrations, then demob, and then Charlie was on the train for home.

CHAPTER 16

The sound of a car horn only feet away from him brought Charlie back to reality. In his nostalgic mood he had sauntered half way over a road junction. An irate young lady driver had sounded her horn and was mouthing something unpleasant to hurry him out of her way. Charlie rested himself on the wall to give his heart a chance to settle down after the turn he had just had. He was just by the door of Ernie Robinson's office. It was one of the few places where Charlie had not been a customer. Ernie sold machines, lathes, and the like to factories and engineering concerns. He wasn't in such a big way now, but there had been a time when he was the talk of Barnforth. He had started with nothing, but had expanded rapidly till he had had one of the most successful businesses in town.

Ernie's mother had been a neighbour of Charlie's, and had always got on well with her, but to tell the truth, Charlie hadn't liked Ernie in his younger days. Even then he had boasted of how he would make 'tons of money'. His own mother summed him up when she said that he had an 'insatiable want'. Ernie had left school at fifteen without any qualifications and had one or two minor sorts of jobs that never lasted very long; consequently he spent quite a lot of time in the dole queue. In the time he had spare he bought old cycles and sold them for a shilling or two extra. He couldn't have made much money at what he was doing, but he suddenly acquired a 'hawker's roll', a roll of money that must have held a hundred, hundred and fifty, even two hundred pounds. It was a fortune, and he flashed it at every opportunity, peeling a note off every time he bought an item. With the roll he also acquired a great deal of confidence. He also acquired the nickname Millionaire Ern.

Charlie was in the White Swan one Friday evening at a table with a group of acquaintances, one of whom was Henshaw the butcher. The dominoes were on the table but no one was playing, for Henshaw was a loud mouthed braggart, a twister, a boaster, and always had a couple of henchmen in tow. Ernie Robinson walked into the pub and bought a packet of ten cigarettes. As usual he pulled out his roll to pay for them, changed his mind, and paid with the loose change in his pocket.

Old Sam Stonehouse was drinking a half pint of beer at the bar. He said to Ernie, 'Come on, lad, are you going to sit down and see if we can take a couple of shillings off you in a game of dominoes?'

'Now, if you would make it a fiver, I might be interested,' Ernie replied jokingly.

Henshaw the butcher slammed a five pound note on the table. 'Sit yourself down there, lad, and let's see what you're made of.'

His henchman rose from the chair, and Ernie had no choice: he had to sit down and play.

'First one with three chalks on the board wins, OK lad?'

Ernie paled and nodded his head. Henshaw was a shrewd man and a good domino player; even if he played fair he would have won easily, but as Fred Harding said, 'He couldn't lie straight in bed.' His henchman took up station behind Ernie, and by a system of simple signs conveyed to Henshaw the dominoes in Ernie's hand. Rubbing his forehead indicated double six, rubbing his nose meant double five, rubbing his chin meant double four. They were well known signs. To a good domino player it was the only information needed to secure a win.

Ernie lost three chalks to nil. Charlie was seated right next to him. He didn't feel sorry for Ernie losing his five pounds, in fact he thought it served him right for being so blatant with his money. Ernie pulled his roll from his pocket, but this time kept it under the table where only his own and Charlie's eyes could see it. He peeled off a pound note, and two ten shilling notes, and that was all there was; the rest of the roll was plain paper cut to the size of pound notes and held together with two elastic bands.

Charlie instantly saw a different Ernie Robinson, an ordinary lad with nothing, the same as everyone else, but so desperate to get on and be someone that he was prepared to go to these lengths to achieve his goal. If his ruse was discovered, as it was about to be, he would be the laughing stock of the town and would never regain his confidence. Charlie only had three pound notes in his pocket. He quickly put them on the table and said to Ernie, 'Here's the three pounds back that I borrowed from you the other day, it'll save breaking too far into your roll.'

'Thank you, Charlie, I'd forgotten about that.' Ernie put his two pounds with Charlie's three, and pushed them over the table to Henshaw. Ernie left the pub with his image intact. At seven o'clock the following morning Ernie was in Charlie's house. He handed the three pounds back to Charlie.

'Charlie, I can't thank you enough for what you did for me last night. I didn't mean any harm to anybody, it's just when I've got nothing I don't get any respect, and you know when I'm buying and selling and people know I've no money it's awful hard to make a deal.'

'It's all right, lad, I know what it's all about. Now forget it. I have.'

Soon after that Ernie obtained a job with Williamson's; they were machine tool suppliers about two miles out of town. They had an awful reputation of loyalty to their work people, especially to their counter staff, usually keeping them only till they were twenty years old, letting them go before they came on to full rate of pay. Ernie enjoyed the job, as being on the counter meant he had contact with the customers. He tried to help in any way he could, and felt certain that the customers appreciated what he did for them. Unlike Williamson's bosses who treated him with disregard, and if the counter wasn't too busy he was given all the menial tasks expected of an underling.

One morning Ernie was directed to the office, where there were papers to dispose of. He put them all in a cardboard box and took them to a corner of the yard to incinerate them, but before burning them he looked them over. There were out of date customer lists, and price lists from suppliers. Ernie was amazed at the profit margins on a lot of articles. He looked out some of the more interesting lists, put them in to his bait-bag, and took them home.

True to form Ernie was given his marching orders a week before his twentieth birthday. Ernie used these lists to his advantage. He contacted the machine tool suppliers, and made an arrangement with them to supply machine tools to any customer he could find. He then acquired an old car and travelled round Williamson's customers, acquired from the other salvaged list. From working on the counter, he knew a lot of the customers, most of whom he had helped. Some of them gave him small orders, which he personally ensured were delivered promptly.

The business he had started flourished, and expanded rapidly. In weeks he had an office in town, with a girl of about his age looking after it. He didn't carry stock, but just acted as agent to the big machine tool suppliers; consequently he was able to give discounts to his customers, which in turn brought in more business. He then expanded into the second-hand market. In different parts of the country, some machine tools were more popular than others, and by studying these areas carefully he found a very lucrative market. He was at last making his 'tons of money'.

In a few months he married Julie, the girl who looked after the office for him. Within the year they had a baby girl. Over the next fifteen years Ernie's 'insatiable want' came even more to the fore. How Julie stood it, no one knew. However much his business turned over it was never enough; he stopped only to sleep, constantly driving himself on, chasing all over the country seeking more and more business. His home life was led at the same breakneck pace. In their short married life they must have lived in eighteen to twenty houses. They would just become settled in a house when Ernie would get his eye on another which was just a little better, and a little more expensive, and they would move again. It was the same with his cars. He would have the top of the range in one model, but after a few months it would have to be changed for the top of the range in another marque. His daughter's schooling was carried on in the same vein. She was in private school, but she never had a chance to settle. Ernie frequently found a better, more expensive school, and she would move on.

It wasn't humanly possible to keep going at such a pace. The beginning of his troubles came one evening when hurrying home to prepare another big deal. A young lad delivering papers on his bicycle swerved across the road in front of him. The bag holding the papers had jammed in the front wheel. If Ernie had been travelling at a reasonable speed he would have been able to avoid the paper boy, but as he was going at probably twice the speed limit, he didn't have a chance of missing him. The boy was badly hurt: broken leg, broken ribs, broken cheek bone and severe grazing. The police and the ambulance were on the scene very quickly, and Ernie soon found himself making a statement to a burly policeman of about fifty years old. Ernie's salesman brain worked quickly; he saw no point in accepting the blame. He would buy the lad a new bike and give him a couple of hundred pounds when he came out of hospital. He lied to the policeman on how fast he had been going; there were no immediate witnesses, and no tell-tale skid marks on the road.

On completion of the statement the policeman passed it to Ernie to sign. As he reached for the pen it slipped from the policeman's hand. They both stopped to pick it up, and with a speed that belied his bulk the policeman was down before Ernie. As he straightened up he brought his elbow hard into Ernie's solar plexus. The pain was intense, he was verging on unconsciousness; there must have been a dozen or more witnesses in close proximity yet the policeman had been so clever with the blow that no one had seen anything untoward. He moved very close to Ernie, and hissed at him, 'You slimy damned toe-rag, we all know who's responsible for this, but don't worry, you'll get away with it. Heed me though: if it's the last thing I do in this world, I'll have you for something.'

The incident weighed heavily on Ernie's mind, but he still kept up the same work-rate. About once a month he made a trip to Bristol, where he always did well, sometimes taking orders into the hundreds of thousands of pounds. Not content with that, when he stopped for breakfast he was on the telephone arranging a deal with two firms in different parts of the country. He was trading a secondhand metal bending machine. By the time he put the telephone down he had made himself ten thousand pounds on the deal.

From first thing that morning, Ernie had had a sensation in his chest. He hadn't thought of it as a pain until he was carrying his breakfast tray to a table, when he thought to himself, 'This pain is getting worse.' Then the heart attack hit him. It was like being hit in the chest with a battering ram. He fell to his knees, the contents of the tray spilling over the floor. Luckily for Ernie there was a doctor in the café. The last thing he remembered was being turned onto his back, the doctor cutting open the sleeve of his £600 suit with a pair of scissors and the sleeve of his £60 shirt.

He felt the prick of the hypodermic needle, and was thrown into another world. He found himself standing in a wilderness of an undulating rough terrain. There was a mountain in the distance with its peak in the clouds and a lake at its foot. Ernie felt a great compulsion to reach the mountain. He felt the need to run, even though he had never run more than twenty yards in his life without running out of breath. He started to run, and it was effortless; his feet hardly seemed to touch the ground. Boulders and chasms were cleared with ease. The mountain was miles in the distance but it wasn't a problem. He was gliding over the ground, and not feeling distress in the least. He was soon at the lakeside. He had never been able to swim, yet he didn't hesitate; he plunged into the water and was swimming with the same ease as he had run over the wilderness. He was obsessed with reaching the mountain: nothing else mattered. Soon he was at the foot of the mountain. He looked up. It was an impossible climb; the face was sheer as far up as he could see. The most experienced of mountaineers would not have attempted it. Ernie hadn't ever done any fell walking; even climbing a ladder was a nerve-racking experience for him. He didn't pause for a moment; he had to make it to the top of the mountain. He reached up and found a hand hold, and again it was easy. He was climbing the sheer face of the mountain without fear or discomfort. He was going up the mountain as a fly would go up a wall.

He was soon in the clouds with nothing to see. It seemed he had been climbing forever. Then suddenly his climb was over; he was on a plateau on the top of the mountain. He could sense there were people there. It was so grey with the low cloud that he couldn't see them, but he knew they were there. He walked a few yards and came to a large table. There was someone sitting at the far side of it, but in the greyness he couldn't make out any features. He was ordered to sit at one of the chairs.

'Ernest Robinson, this is your Heaven. It is the Heaven you have created for yourself in your lifetime. There is nothing here for you, but it is your eternity. There are people of your like here, but you can't communicate with them. There is nothing here, no pain, no pleasure; no day, no night; no hot, no cold; no wet, no dry; no men, no women; no light, no dark; nothing to have, nothing to give; no beauty, no ugliness; nothing to win, nothing to lose.'

Ernie had heard enough. He rose from the chair and walked back to the edge of the plateau, intending to climb back down. He had only walked a few yards, but he couldn't find the plateau's edge. He turned back to the table, but couldn't find his way back to it. All he could do was walk in the greyness. He could only see a yard or two, and could only barely see the ground he walked upon hence he had to concentrate continually in case he walked into something. He was afraid, and felt panic. It was horrendous, as he tried to settle himself to an eternity of endless wandering.

Then he heard voices, and saw bright lights in front of his closed eyes. He forced them open, and found himself in an intensive therapy ward. The sister in charge of the ward was smiling and standing over him; his wife Julie was sitting by his side holding his hand. The sister spoke to him.

'It's good to have you back with us, Mr Robinson. We thought we had lost you, we had to resuscitate you twice, once in the ambulance and again when we admitted you to the ward. Lucky that doctor was at hand when you collapsed.' She held his other hand and smiled into his eyes. 'You've been on the brink you know, right on the edge.'

Ernie smiled at Julie and the nurse and thought to himself, 'I've been further than that; I've been over the edge.'

A couple of days later he was in the normal ward and recovering slowly. The heart specialist had a long talk with Ernie, explaining to him that he had had a severe heart-attack, but by being sensible and altering his life-style, given time there was no reason why he shouldn't make a full recovery. Ernie promised, and meant it, that he would follow all the advice he was given.

Ernie was soon discharged from the hospital and taken home by Julie to convalesce. Ernie's business still flourished, but not at its previous high pressure rate. The experience he had been through had frightened him so much it made him appreciate his home-life much more. He was more content with what he had; his 'insatiable want' was past.

CHAPTER 17

L ooking to the other side of the road, Charlie took in the imposing stone building that was the home of the High Street Bank. Charlie had been a very disillusioned customer. Coming home from the Services after the war had been a traumatic time of his life. He and his intended wife Lilly had been apart so long that they felt strange in each other's company. The closeness they had had was gone, so much so that Charlie was looking for excuses to cool their relationship. He hinted to his mother that maybe she needed him home to take care of things for her. She nearly snapped his head off, and told him to sort himself out. She had been alone for the most of five years, and had grown used to it.

'I've no intention of wet nursing you again,' she said sternly. 'You have a lovely young woman who has waited patiently for you for five years. Give yourself a shake, lad, and take a bit of responsibility. Make a home for Lilly and yourself.'

It wasn't just his relationship with Lilly that was upsetting him. The thought of returning to the foundry also filled him with dread. They were obliged to take him back, but it was so different now. There were few of his former work-mates left. Some had retired, some hadn't returned from the war, and others like him just didn't fancy that type of work any more. He thought he might try to find work as a lorry driver, but it was difficult. The firms he spoke to were looking for drivers with experience. They were dubious about Service drivers.

It was Lilly who put the idea into his head when she said, 'Why don't you buy a lorry and go into business for yourself? I have a bit of money put by which would help you get started.'

Charlie slept on it, and the idea grew on him. He had made an allowance to his mother all the time he had been in the RAF, and she hadn't spent a penny of it, but had kept it for him for when he came home. With that money, and the money Lilly had saved he had nearly

£500 available to him.

He became quite excited about the project. Even his forthcoming marriage was not so daunting; after all, they did have their own house that would soon become available. The family who had rented it from them belonged to the Channel Islands, and would soon be going home. During the war years Lilly had gathered together the basic furniture they would require, so there would be very little expense needed in that department, and their wedding would be fundamental to say the least, as after the war resources were limited: even if they had a packet of money to spend, supplies, especially foodstuffs, were unobtainable. In Charlie's mind the £500 was ample to see them married, and set up in the haulage business. His enthusiasm rubbed off onto Lilly and they slowly grew together again.

Lilly was relieved when Charlie began to show enthusiasm again. She had felt the lessening keenness in him. It had been one of her better moves, suggesting he start his own business. The next few months were the busiest in his life; they organised their wedding and timed it for when their house would be empty. Between times he began to set up his impending business.

It wasn't as easy as it had seemed. Buying the lorry was the easy part. He found a decent secondhand one for £200. Then the difficulties started. He hadn't had the lorry a day before the authorities were on to him. There was a bye-law whereby a business couldn't be run from the street, which, as the official pointed out, meant that the lorry couldn't stand outside Charlie's door. This was the point where his friendship with Fred Harding was re-kindled, though they had lost touch in the war years. Fred knew a coalman who had recently retired, and had his coal-yard up for sale. It was the ideal place for Charlie, only a five minute walk from his house and with a close-boarded fence around its perimeter. Two hundred and fifty pounds was the least price the retired coalman would take. It was an expense Charlie could have done without, but it was a case of needs must, so he made the deal. A sinking feeling in Charlie's stomach told him the capital he had was insufficient to turn the business that was in his mind into reality.

That was the first setback; there were others to follow. To carry goods for profit meant his lorry had to be appropriately licensed. There were two categories of licence: the A and the B. The A Licence was virtually impossible to obtain unless it was bought from another haulage contractor, and the price would be phenomenal, way out of Charlie's reach. The other option, the B Licence, was a tonnage in a twenty-five mile radius of home; this was not quite so difficult to obtain, but it did mean applying to the local Court. Charlie consulted a solicitor, who agreed to represent him in Court. The solicitor advised him that it was by no means cut and dried that he would be granted the licence. He would need letters from firms who would promise him work, and even then other haulage contractors would object, saying they had enough lorries to manage the work that was available.

It was a worrying time for Charlie; his money was rapidly running out and he was nowhere near ready to earn with his lorry. Even when he was, it would be a while before he was paid for his work. His marriage was looming ever closer, and that was going to be more costly than he had budgeted for. The proprietors of the foundry were a help to him in his approaching Court hearing; they gave him a letter promising him work with his lorry if his licence was granted, but in the back of his mind he had the feeling that they were pleased he wasn't coming back as a full time employee, at not having to honour their obligations.

He discussed his predicament with Lilly, and they decided he would have to approach the bank, and ask for a loan. It couldn't have been easier. The bank manager took him into his office, and they discussed his needs. The bank manager was very knowledgeable on all aspects of business, and came up with all manner of expenses that Charlie hadn't even thought of. Between them they came up with the figure of £800 he would need to borrow to see him married, set up in a home, and his haulage business up and running.

'Don't worry,' the manager said to him. 'We will loan you the money; you have plenty of security in your house and yard to cover it. We will make the money available to you in the form of an overdraft so you will only draw the money as you need it; that way you won't be paying for money you don't need.'

Charlie's worries were eased. He and Lilly were married; they moved into their house, and set up their home. His licence was granted by the Court, although he was a bit embarrassed when his solicitor made great play on his exemplary war service. This did undoubtedly influence the magistrate, but the main sway, Charlie thought, was the promise of work from the foundry.

Setting up home fell on Lilly's willing shoulders. She cleaned, decorated and painted their house, and made it the way she wanted it. The arrangement suited Charlie, for his time and attention were fully taken up with his haulage enterprise. It took three years and, as the bank manager had predicted, the most of £800 before his business was running smoothly, three years that passed so quickly that he could barely believe it, but he became used to being in debt. He was earning enough for them to live comfortably, pay the interest, and keep paying a part of the loan back to the bank. One of the years he made a real effort to bring the borrowing down, denying himself and Lilly every little extravagance they had enjoyed, but at the end of it he was no better off. He was landed with a tax bill for £250. The whole exercise had been worthless to him.

With the business taking up so much of his time, he missed out a lot on family life. Within a year of being married they had a son, or to be more precise, Lilly had a son. Charlie was not the doting father that he might have been in different circumstances, for, as Lilly put it so many times, he was quite content to leave the baby to 'God and good neighbours'. What Charlie was lacking in fatherhood, Lilly more than made up with her mothering. She called the baby Charles after his father, but insisted that it never be shortened to 'Charlie'. The baby became her whole life, so much so that Charlie felt quite downrated, sometimes even a twinge jealous.

Things were going well, and Charlie was ready to expand the business. An acquaintance was retiring who was in the same line of business as Charlie, and an arrangement was made between them for Charlie to take over one of his lorries. The deal was that Charlie would give him a hundred pounds, and take over the hire purchase agreement on one of his nearly new lorries. With it came a contract to lead stone for the quarry. Charlie signed papers to this effect, the deal to come about in a month. He even had a driver promised to start on that date.

Then came what Charlie thought was a hiccup, but which turned out to be a bombshell. His lorry developed a fault; a seal in the engine failed and when the engine stopped the water was able to mix with the oil. He was still able to use the lorry providing he stopped every half-hour and filled it with water, and at night when he was finished work he had to drain the water to prevent it mixing with the oil.

Obviously he couldn't go on like this. He called at the garage that did his repairs and was quoted £270 to renew the engine and to do a few other necessary jobs.

Before giving the go-ahead for the work, he decided to visit the bank and arrange to borrow a little more money to help him over the next few months. Unbeknown to Charlie, however, the manager he had dealt with had been a little too liberal with the bank's money, and had made loans that some customers had been unable to repay. The bank hierarchy had moved the over-generous manager on, and had replaced him with a much more stringent character. He was there to tighten up the ship, as the saying goes, and Charlie was to be one of his victims. From the moment he walked into the new manager's office he had a feeling of apprehension; he was sure if the new manager had had Scrooge for a customer he would have accused him of being a spendthrift, throwing his money about on frivolities like Christmas bonuses and such.

The new manager sat and listened to Charlie's proposal, and said to him, 'I'll have to deliberate this matter very carefully. I need to consult a higher authority, so I can't give you an answer immediately, but I'll be as quick as I can. I'll write to you and inform you of our decision in the very near future. Good-day to you.'

The promised letter was on the door mat the following morning. It knocked all the wind from Charlie's sails. Not only would they not loan him the extra money, they also insisted that the original overdraft be repaid within the month, and they reminded him that his share of the house, and his yard, were held as securities. They would demand their sale to settle his debt.

This was the only letter he had received since their marriage that he didn't show to Lilly. She was taking Charles to a newly opened holiday camp for a fortnight. A group of wives from their street had organised the holiday. Sixteen mothers and their children were going, and had a small bus hired to take them. This was one of the reasons why Charlie didn't tell her, he didn't want to spoil their holiday; the other reason was that he just didn't know how to break the news to her or what he was going to do.

The haulage business was very competitive, and if it became known that he was in financial distress the rates for his work would be cut so close that he would be lucky to survive. If he sold up, all he would have to sell was a broken-down lorry, its licence, and his yard. Some of his customers were bad payers and only paid when they needed another job doing. If he were out of business they would never pay him.

Charlie struggled on for most of a week. It was bad enough with the lorry being in such bad condition; the financial worries on top of it all just added to his miseries. He worked out his resources in a dozen different ways, and each time the answer was the same. If the bank sold him up he would be at least £600 to the bad. What would happen to their house he didn't dare think about.

About three o'clock on the Friday afternoon, feeling as miserable as sin, he was travelling back to his yard with his lorry empty. He stopped outside the High Colliery to put water in the engine. The colliery had run into a geological fault, and had been forced to close down. Charlie knew there was a salvage team working there. The foreman of the team came striding over, just as Charlie was preparing to move off. The man was furious, and had a foul mouth. Charlie couldn't understand what was wrong with the fellow, and it didn't help matters when the foreman pointed to his wrist and screamed, 'What do you call this, then?'

Charlie, never one to be intimidated, said, 'Looks like a wrist watch to me.'

Charlie thought the foreman was going to burst. 'A comedian, eh! God knows there's no shortage of comedians around here. You know full well that we have to be in Sheffield to-morrow. Get across into the colliery yard and let's have the job finished.'

Charlie racked his brains. In the mental state he had been in had he forgotten a job he had promised to do? In trying to remember, he wasn't concentrating on what he was doing. There were six men standing by a heap of metal. Charlie drove over to them as directed, and before he knew what was happening they were furiously throwing the metal onto his lorry. Within quarter of an hour the metal was all transferred on his lorry, a form was pushed under Charlie's nose, he scribbled his signature on it, and the salvage gang were in the van and on the road to Sheffield.

Charlie was flummoxed; all he could do was drive back to his yard. By the time he arrived the lorry was boiling like a steam kettle. He reckoned it was well overloaded, and cursed as he scalded his fingers when he opened the valve to let the water run from the engine.

His heart skipped a beat when he examined the load; it was scrap copper, and worth a fortune. He was frightened and didn't know what to do, so pulled a tarpaulin over it and made his way home. There was no sleep for him that night; he had visions of policemen at his door, to question him on how he came to be in possession of a load of scrap copper. He turned the situation over in his mind. He hadn't stolen it, he decided, but that wouldn't be how the police would view it.

Saturday morning was his maintenance time for his lorry. He unlocked his yard gate and tentatively raised the tarpaulin, half hoping his lorry was empty and that it had all been a bad dream, but not so: the scrap copper was still there. He half-heartedly greased the lorry, unable to keep his attention away from the gate. He was expecting a hue and cry to erupt at any minute. Nothing happened. He re-locked the gate, and spent two sessions at the White Swan. If the scrap copper was being looked for, someone in the pub would know of it, and it would be gossiped over, but it was never mentioned.

Saturday night he slept better, and on Sunday he didn't even look into his yard. With Lilly still on holiday, he was lonely, and missing her. He filled in his time by having another two sessions at the White Swan.

Monday morning he didn't feel too good, which was understandable considering the amount of beer he had consumed over the week-end. With his lorry being in poor condition he hadn't taken any work on; he didn't hurry to his yard, so it must have been about ten o'clock when he arrived. When he saw the lorry, all the apprehensions came back to him; the illicit load was still there where he had left it. He looked at it for a while, and made his mind up what he would do. It had to come off the lorry. He knew of a new scrap merchant who had set up business well out of town; there was always a lot of activity going on at this scrap yard, so Charlie thought it showed he must be a fair merchant. He would take the load of scrap copper to him. He made the lorry ready, started up, and pulled out of his yard. He had to pass the site of the High Colliery, but it was deserted, not a soul in sight. About half a mile from the scrap yard, he stopped and refilled the lorry with water; he wanted it to look decent when he arrived.

The scrap yard was much bigger than Charlie had thought, with mountains of scrap iron. He was directed onto a weigh-bridge, and a young chap came over from the office.

'What have you for us to-day, then?' he asked.

'I have a load of copper I want to sell.'

The young fellow looked in the lorry, and whistled through his teeth. 'I'll have to bring the boss to look at this.'

Charlie's heart sank, had something been said, were they looking for a load of stolen scrap copper? After an agonising five minutes the boss came over. He was younger than Charlie and much over-weight, but nevertheless climbed up and looked in the lorry.

'You've picked the right time to bring copper in, there's a world shortage at the minute. Providing it's clean stuff right through, I'll give you top money for it.'

The load was tipped off, he examined it again, gave it his approval, and said, 'Come with me to the office, and we'll settle up.' He did a quick calculation, and wrote out a sales slip. 'Comes to £1,925. If you take this slip to the other office, Sally will pay you out.'

Charlie couldn't believe his ears; he had thought two maybe three hundred; he had never dreamt it could be as much as this. His legs were shaking as he entered the other office, and he wasn't concentrating.

'I can let you have up to a hundred in cash, the rest'll have to be in a cheque; that all right with you, Sunshine?'

Charlie grinned at the cheeky-faced Sally; she had brought him back to reality.

'Just let me have the twenty-five in cash; a cheque will do fine for the rest.'

It was manna from Heaven. He drove straight to the garage and gave instructions for repairs to his lorry, walked to the bank and deposited the cheque. He saw the manager's name on his office door: it was Mr Goodman. 'That's not what I'd call you,' thought Charlie. He then walked round and made the final arrangements for the lorry he was to buy, and was just in time for the first session at the White Swan.

The following morning there was another letter from the bank, stating how good a customer he was, and that they would be pleased to restore his overdraft facilities. Charlie tore up both letters, and burned them. He looked forward to Lilly coming home from the holiday camp; she would never know the trauma he had been through. He made up his mind he would buy Lilly, Charles and his mother new winter overcoats.

Even after so many years the incident was still fresh in Charlie's mind. If the bank had been reasonable with him, he might have made it big in the haulage business; he had been in it at just the right time for it to have really taken off. He would never put his faith in the bank again. He would never go through the agony of that fortnight again for anyone. Without the pressure from the bank, deep in his heart he knew he would never have kept the load of scrap copper; he blamed them for making him a thief. Sometimes when his spirits were down feelings still came over him that made him feel a criminal. He shook his head as he gazed at the bank building and thought, 'Yes, I've been a customer there.'

CHAPTER 18

R ight next door to the bank was Williamson's Garage. Charlie had been a customer there for a lot of years, buying most of the fuel for his two lorries from Joe Williamson. Joe had bought the garage just after the war, at about the same time as Charlie had set himself up in the haulage business. When Joe had bought the business they were tiny premises, serving fuel over the pavement by means of a gantry. It was primitive, to say the least. He had moved to Barnforth from Moulton West, a village a few miles out of town. The business was very different now, however, and was no longer called a garage. It had expanded into a huge motor complex with a forecourt, a showroom that sold prestigious cars and a service department, all run with a smooth efficiency by their respective managers. Charlie gazed at the showroom for a while, contemplating whether or not to call in. If old Joe Williamson was in, Charlie was assured of a welcome. He would be given a cup of coffee laced with whisky, a fancy cream cake, and perhaps an expensive cigar to smoke later. If it was Mrs Williamson who was in, or the son or daughter, Charlie wouldn't be given the time of day.

Charlie could well remember when Joe first came to Barnforth. He didn't have it easy. It was a one-man business, doing motor repairs in the garage; and having to drop everything if a customer came for fuel. He wasn't an easy man to become friendly with, his shyness was taken by many to be standoffish, but Charlie as a regular customer came to know him well. On the other hand, his wife was very out-going, and quickly became part of the community; with a young son and daughter at Infant School she took the opportunity to join the social side of her daughter's activities. Her mother was a regular visitor and spent most of her time under Joe's roof.

One evening Charlie was sitting in the White Swan with Fred and a few more friends when Joe opened the door and walked in. One of the

Ladies' Group was having a meeting, and it was Joe's wife's turn to do the entertaining, enthusiastically assisted by her mother. Joe had been obliged to go out. Walking into the White Swan for the first time was a bit of an ordeal, especially for anyone alone. There was always a hush, and everyone looked at the stranger. Charlie saved Joe's embarrassment by calling him over to where they were playing dominoes, and after a couple of glasses of beer Joe turned out to be quite good company. This happened increasingly; as Joe's wife became more popular with the Ladies' Group, Joe's house was called on to host ever more meetings.

Charlie could remember the last night that Joe was ever in the White Swan. Charlie and Fred were in, and as usual Joe joined their company. There was a fellow in the pub, Ollie Smithers, who had just won thirty-five pounds on the horses, and was throwing his money about buying drinks for his cronies. Charlie and Fred didn't usually associate with him, but they had no qualms, they would toast anyone's good fortune. With a little enticing from Charlie, Joe too joined the group. It resulted in them having three or four glasses of whiskey over their usual amount. It loosened Joe's tongue, and after turning-out time he and Charlie stood talking on the street corner.

'Charlie, I'll tell you straight, I've had just about enough. I'm seriously thinking of leaving my lot, garage, family, everything. My business, Charlie, as I'm sure you will understand, doesn't leave a lot of money. I have to work damned hard for every penny, but I can't make the wife and family understand this; she spends like money's going out of fashion. I can't go on like this, Charlie, and to top it all, do you know, she thinks more of her Ladies' Clubs than she does of me and the business. Her mother is always there, sticking her nose in. The top and bottom of it is, they are too toffee nosed, they think the garage is beneath them, they are even twisting when I take my overalls in the house. None of them would dream of coming out and serving a customer with a gallon of petrol. But I'll tell you what happened to-night that's upset me the most, and for me it's the last straw, it really epitomizes the whole situation.

'We were having pork chops for dinner. I was washing my hands, and the chops were standing by the cooker waiting to be cooked. There were four beauties, and one off the scrag-end, discoloured, three parts fat, and had a blue mark on the rind. I know people who would hesitate to feed a chop like that to their dog. Do you know, Charlie, I knew as soon as I looked at it who would be served that chop, and I was right: it was mine. There's going to be some straight talking, Charlie, and things will change drastically or I'm off back to Moulton West, 'cos if not, as I've said, I'm off.'

Charlie took a close look at Joe, whose eyes were turning a bit glassy. His speech too was a bit slurred, and he was starting to stagger. Charlie realised what was happening: the cool night air was enhancing the effect of the alcohol. He decided he would have to see Joe safely home. By the time they arrived, Joe was slightly more than intoxicated, and singing 'Land of Hope and Glory' loudly and off key. The Ladies' Meeting was in the process of breaking up, the more important members just taking their leave; they were not impressed with Joe's condition. Miss Newberry, the biggest prude in town, was framed in the living-room doorway, looking down her pointed nose in a most disapproving manner. It was the middle of April, but Joe grinned at her, shouted 'Happy New Year!' and made a beeline to her, presumably to kiss her. Luckily he fell over the door-mat, and fell in a heap at her feet. Charlie helped him back onto his shaky legs and guided him into the kitchen. His wife made tea for him and Charlie, to dilute the alcohol, she said. It worked; slowly Joe sobered up and sat there, looking very sorry for himself. All the while his mother-in-law hovered, her face like thunder.

It was time for Charlie to take his leave. When he got as far as the kitchen door, Joe called to him, 'Thanks for listening, Charlie, you're a good mate!'

As his wife opened the front door to let Charlie out she gave him a very quizzical look.

The following evening was the annual Farmers' and Tradesmen's Ball, an elaborate name for a charity fund-raising buffet and dance. Charlie had bought two tickets for the event, with the intention of Lilly and himself having the evening out. His reasons for wanting to attend were two-fold: the main reason was to have a social evening with Lilly, but he also had a customer, William Storey, whom he had done quite a lot of work for, and who owed him a fair amount of money. William was not a bad payer, but as he refused to use the post, the only way to be paid was to see him. Calling at his premises was a sure way of collecting the money, but William was a good talker. If Charlie called he would lose half a day. He knew William would be at the dance, so there was a good chance of having a word with him, and collecting his money.

At the last minute Lilly cried off. Charles had developed a sniffle, and she refused to leave him with a neighbour. They had a few cross words over the situation, but Lilly wouldn't budge. Charlie was obliged to attend by himself. Being alone, he only intended staying long enough to collect his dues; he would then go along to the White Swan and finish the evening there. He walked into the hall, made his way to the bar, and bought himself a glass of beer. His luck was in. William Storey called him over.

'A good chance for us to settle up, Charlie, eh!'

'Thanks very much, William, that's much appreciated.'

Within ten minutes of being there, Charlie had his cheque safely in his pocket; he would finish his glass of beer, and be on his way. He had only taken a couple of sips when, as he looked round the hall, he made eye to eye contact with Joe Williamson, the garage owner, who beckoned Charlie over to join him. Joe was sitting at a table with his wife, his mother-in-law, and two ladies from one of the Ladies' Clubs accompanied by their husbands, the Walker brothers, who were fruit and potato merchants. Charlie sat down at the table with them. He didn't know the Walker brothers, but he had heard of them, and from the reports he had they were a boasting, cunning pair. Charlie hadn't been at the table for five minutes when one of them made to pick up his glass. 'Let me put you another half in there, Charlie,' he said, but Charlie was too experienced a hand to be caught like that; he would soon have to buy a round for the whole table if he accepted. He clamped his hand onto his glass and gave him an emphatic no, making the excuse he wouldn't be staying long.

The Walker brothers were the only two in the Hall, other than the MC, who were in bow ties and evening suits. Charlie wasn't keen on them from the first introduction, and before long this had turned to a distinct dislike. Charlie knew there was a glut of potatoes that year, and it was becoming late in the season. Farmers were becoming desperate to sell their remaining stocks. One such farmer that Charlie occasionally did work for had asked him if he knew any merchant who was buying potatoes. Charlie had told him he had seen the Walker brothers moving stocks. The farmer's blunt reply was, 'I'd rather throw them in the pond.' Having now met them, he could understand the farmer's attitude. Apparently the price of potatoes was set by the Government, the farmers not allowed to charge more than the fixed price and the merchants not allowed to pay less. In the potato glut the way round this was for the farmer to give instead of twenty bags to the ton, twenty-one or two, or even twenty-three bags to the ton. This was the topic of conversation at the table. The Walker brothers were naming farmers, and boasting how many bags to the ton they were taking from them. Charlie was fuming, for he knew a lot of the farmers who were being mentioned. The only times they weren't boasting was when they were buttering up Joe Williamson's wife and mother-in-law, who were visibly purring with their attentions. Their motives were so blatant. When it was their turn to buy a round of drinks, it was half beers for themselves and half shandies for the ladies, but when it was Joe's turn, at his wife's instigation they would have a 'proper' drink: gin, whisky, rum or brandy, and all with expensive mixers.

What they were doing was so obvious and so loathesome that Charlie's blood was boiling. Perhaps what Joe had told him the previous evening had not been just the drink talking. Joe's wife's standing and popularity in the community was showing through; she was never short of conversation or offers to dance, with his mother-in-law overlooking the situation with smug approval. Joe could only sit through the proceedings, spoken to only when he was required to buy an expensive round of drinks. Charlie was uncomfortable in their company, and only stayed because he felt sorry for Joe and thought he needed his support.

After the buffet had been served, three strangers came into the hall, a young fellow a few years younger than Charlie, accompanied by two lovely looking young ladies, well groomed, and delightfully dressed. They were striking young ladies and were so classy they attracted a lot of attention. Even one of the Walker brothers commented, 'How does a chap get an introduction to someone like that?'

After the buffet break the band returned to the stage and the MC took the microphone. He said, 'Ladies and Gentlemen, the bandleader has informed me that it is now time for the latest dance innovation; he calls it the "Jam" session. He tells me that this type of dancing will soon take over our dances. I don't believe him, but let's show him we are game for a stab at it. So it's either Ladies' Choice, or Gentlemen's Choice, or if there's not enough of you on the floor, it'll have to be my choice. So, Ladies and Gentlemen, a quickstep to warm you up, and then into the "Jam" session.'

The band struck up with a quickstep, and out of the corner of his eye Charlie caught sight of one of the female strangers walking towards him. His heart sank, he thought she was going to ask him to dance, but she walked straight past him and held her two hands out to Joe. Without a word between them, Joe accompanied her onto the dance floor. He didn't even excuse himself from the company he was in. The band upped the tempo. Charlie couldn't believe his eyes: Joe and the stranger put on an exhibition of dancing that Charlie had only seen at the cinema. Their movement was lovely to watch as they went through every move in the book. She rolled over his hips and his back, even swung between his legs. It was a marvellous exhibition. The other dancers on the floor stood back and clapped.

When the dance was over, Charlie and the rest of the crowd whistled and cheered them off the floor. Everyone, that is, except the company that Joe and Charlie had been in, who were sitting in stoney silence. Joe didn't return to the table but joined the strangers at the end of the bar, and motioned Charlie over to join them.

They were lively company, and Charlie soon learned a little about them. They were from Moulton West, and had called to hear the band with a view to hiring them for a forthcoming event. The two girls were sisters, Rachel and Constance. Rachel was married to the young man who was accompanying them. To Charlie the most astonishing fact was that Constance and Joe had been radar specialists in the war and had both been stationed at a large American base. Dances had been the most popular entertainment, and there had been at least one a week, sometimes two or three. Constance had been Joe's regular partner at these dances, and with 'Jive', and 'Jitterbug' being paramount this is where they had learned the moves to be so proficient in the 'Jam' session. They must have stood talking and laughing for a half hour or more.

Charlie kept stealing a glance at the table, and every time he did he saw Joe's wife glowering back at him. 'If looks could kill,' he thought.

It was the turning point in Joe's business. His wife turned out and served petrol, the Ladies' Clubs faded into the background, his mother-in-law's presence became ever less and her influence faded, and the business started to grow. Surrounding properties were acquired, an office was established which Joe's wife took control of, and over the years the Motor Complex had developed. It was a compliment to their co-operation. Charlie had been in on their turning point, privy to their watershed, as it were. He was the thorn in Joe's wife's side; she positively emanated antagonism towards him, whereas Joe was just the opposite.

Charlie grinned to himself. The situation had always amused him. He wouldn't call today, he wasn't quite in the mood, but he made a mental note that he would call on another day.

CHAPTER 19

Life for Charlie became a lot easier when his mind settled as the affair with the bank and the scrap copper faded into the background. The scrap, incidentally, was never missed; Charlie never even heard it mentioned. The second lorry was a success, and the arrangement with the quarry meant permanent work for his employee, who was a pleasant young chap. The money from the contract paid both their wages, the hire-purchase debt, and the maintenance and running costs of the two lorries. He had the opportunity to buy a coach, and expand into that line of business. The coach would have come with a driver and a good contract. Lilly called him a 'stick in the mud' when he refused it, but she didn't know of the troubles he had had with the bank.

It saddened him that Lilly and he lived such separate lives, she taken up with the house and Charles, and he with his lorries and his business. The only social life they had together was the odd Saturday evening at the cinema. They had many differences of opinion on how Charles should be brought up. Charlie thought he should be allowed out more, to play and make more friends. Lilly insisted he make more of school, and spend regular time doing homework. They were differences Lilly always won.

He mentioned the situation to Fred one evening in the White Swan and to Charlie's dismay, Fred took Lilly's part.

'Charlie, it's turning into a different world these days, different to when we were lads. In future it's not what you do that's going to earn the money, it's what you know. So you leave it your Lilly, and take my word for it, don't interfere.' It was Charlie firmly put in place on that score.

Charlie was forty-eight years old when his mother died; thankfully she didn't suffer like his sister Hannah had. He had usually managed to call on his mother most days, so she was a big miss to him when she died. He had called on the Wednesday lunchtime, and she had been right as rain. Thursday morning a neighbour sent a message that his mother wasn't feeling too good. Charlie hurried over to her house. She had had a stroke, the doctor told him. She was conscious, and spoke to him.

The doctor said to Charlie when they were out of earshot, 'We will have to leave her in bed, we can't get her up, for she has no feeling down her left side. I fear the stroke is still working on her so we will just keep her warm and quiet, and I will be back this afternoon. We will make a decision then as to whether she needs to be in hospital.'

Charlie stayed all day, and watched as his mother lapsed into unconsciousness. The doctor came back in the afternoon, but it was obvious that it was pointless taking her into hospital. Ten o'clock that night she died. Charlie grieved. It hurt him to think that he was the last in his family's line, apart from his son Charles.

Charlie made many acquaintances in his line of work, all of them with very different characters, some humorous, others dour, but all fitted together to make life's jigsaw interesting. Dealing with these different types of people, keeping his lorries in good condition and up to date, and all that goes with running a business, made the years pass very quickly. He did however often take a nostalgic look back at his RAF days, and think of the interest and excitement that had been part of it. He sometimes thought it had just been a dream, and his time in the Services and the war were unreal. With the mundane tasks of everyday life he often thought the carefree part of his life had ended when he was discharged from the Forces.

Lilly's ideas on education never faltered; she pushed Charles all the way and she never missed a chance to meet his teachers. She would attend every open day, sports day or coffee evening; she took every chance to help in his education. It paid off. Charles won scholarships, first to Grammar school and later to University, and he didn't cost Charlie a penny; even his living expenses were met by a grant. At University, Charles specialised in accountancy, and had came out with a degree and a tremendous letter of recommendation for a future employer from his tutor. At the time when he left University, all young men were expected to do two years' National Service; they were usually called-up at eighteen years of age, but Charles's call-up was deferred until his university course was over.

Charles came home and told his mother and father, 'Even though I have to do my National Service I have been offered a job with a big firm of accountants, I've accepted it because they do a lot in the field of Receivership and Company Liquidation which is my forte. They are even going to sponsor me while I do my Military Service, which means I'll have a proper wage while I'm in the Army.'

'What's all this Receivership and Company Liquidation?' asked Charlie.

'What it means is, if a company can no longer meet its financial commitments we move in, usually at the instigation of a bank or other financial institution, and for a fat fee we either bankrupt the owners and close the firm down, or we try to find a buyer to take the firm over as a going concern.'

Charlie was getting a bit hot under the collar, when he said, 'So whatever happens, the poor fellow who has worked hard and built up the business is taken to the cleaners.'

'Yes, that's about the price of it. It's tough in business today. Some people say of us that we go in when the battle is lost and bayonet the wounded.'

Charlie was fuming; he was remembering how near he had been to being in that position. Lilly was there, so he didn't dare say what was in his mind; he had to content himself with his thoughts. 'I hope they give him the stiffest pair of boots in the British Army, and I hope they march him round the parade ground till he has blisters like pickled onions on all his toes.' Charlie was thwarted even in his thoughts, as Charles was taken into some part of the Diplomatic Corps, and never even issued with a uniform. Lilly was able to show off to the neighbours by showing them letters from Charles, written on official letterheads from British Embassies all over the world.

From his University days, Charles had been friendly with a girl from Kent, which was also the base of the firm of accountants with whom he was to take up a position when his National Service period was over. Naturally he tended to spend the bulk of his available time in that area, resulting in Charlie and Lilly seeing less and less of him. About a month before the end of his National Service he announced his engagement to his girlfriend, Catherine Parker. Her father and mother, Brigadier and

Mrs Parker, invited Charlie and Lilly to spend a day or two with them, and they would have a party to celebrate the occasion. The Parkers were 'as good as gold' with them, but in lifestyles the families were poles apart. The Parkers did their best to entertain them, but the environment was such that Charlie and Lilly felt like 'two ducks in the desert', and were pleased when the celebrations were over and they were able to return home.

A year later Charles and Catherine were to be married in the bride's home town, and again Charlie and Lilly were invited to spend a few days with the Parkers. Remembering the engagement celebrations, they were not looking forward to the ordeal. During the few days they were there, Charlie and Lilly really had their eyes opened to the profound differences in their backgrounds, but Lilly had accomplished her goal: Charles could hold his own with anyone. They were astounded at the circles he was moving in, and with such confidence and ease of manner. They were proud of him, but they knew he no longer belonged to Barnforth. They were grateful to the Parkers for the efforts they made to make them welcome and for entertaining them. Most of all they were delighted at the simple but expensive wedding they provided for the couple. Nevertheless, they were pleased when it was time to leave.

To the world Lilly was proud of Charles, proud that the education she had insisted on had moved him up the social ladder. But in her private moments, Charlie often found her in tears. He did his best to chivvy her out of these moods; he wasn't the most diplomatic person in the world, but Lilly did appreciate his efforts. Slowly she accepted the situation, and in time it had the effect of drawing them closer together, as close even as during their courting days. They shopped together, and had days and evenings out. Charlie could honestly say they were happy together.

In his middle sixties, Charlie was becoming weary. He had worked all his life and he was lucky to have been blessed with good health; he could count on his fingers, practically, the number of days he had lost through illness. Driving every day was an exacting pursuit, though, and it was starting to take its toll on him. On an evening he was becoming more and more like a wrung out dishcloth.

When an offer came along to buy him out, he discussed it with Lilly, and they decided that the money they were to receive from the sale of the business, plus their savings, plus their state pension, would be enough for them to live quite comfortably. The decision made, Charlie sold the business, including his yard and his two lorries, and they officially retired.

They made visits to the local places of interest, and had a holiday each year at various seaside resorts. Their only problem was inflation, as the money they had, which had seemed adequate, was proving not to be; its value was being constantly eroded. One of the last discussions Charlie had had with Fred had been on that subject.

'Do you know, Fred,' Charlie said, 'The first hundred pounds Lilly and I saved would have been worth twenty-five tons of coal. Now, Fred, no one can tell me there is any new coal, they tell me it takes thousands of years to form; now that same hundred pounds will barely buy one ton. It just isn't fair.'

'On that one, Charlie, I agree with you, but that's life, it's just the way it is. If only you had known you would have bought the twenty-five tons, but you wouldn't have been any better off. For one thing, you wouldn't have slept nights worrying in fear someone walked with it, and anyway you'd have burned it by now, so you wouldn't have been any better off.'

'Aye, ah suppose you're right.'

'Aye, an have you noticed, no matter how much we hurry these days, we don't seem to go any faster?'

'Aye, you're right there an all.'

To augment their finances Charlie took a part time job. It was driving a tractor for Alex Brass's son in the busy seasons. It was on the same farm where he had started work when he left school. He even ploughed the same thirty-acre field that had ruined his feet all those years ago, only this time he did it from the comfort of the tractor seat. It was an interest to him, and it kept him from under Lilly's feet. Even now he still called at the farm a couple of times a week; he was always welcome, and was usually invited to lunch. After lunch he loved to take the old collie dog for a walk round the farm. It was good for both him and the dog, because for pace and distance they were about equal; an hour's steady walk was enough for them.

For Lilly the highlight of her year was a visit from Charles and Catherine. She knew it was a perfunctory visit, usually fitted in while they were *en route* to Edinburgh where their firm did quite a lot of business. Barnforth just wasn't Catherine's scene. Of course, she was much too well mannered to say anything derogatory, but it was clearly an ordeal for her. As the years passed by, both Charlie and Lilly thought their son's marriage was going to be childless, but to their surprise and delight, after fifteen years they had two sons within thirteen months. Lilly used all of her available time knitting matinee jackets and pully-ups.

After the sons were born, Charlie began to dread their visits. They were two little rips, always in mischief, and were never chastised: the only punishment they ever received was to be banished to their bedroom, but that would only last about ten minutes, because the mayhem they caused whilst on their own was usually worse than what they were being punished for in the first place. Fred summed them up one afternoon when he visited when they were there: 'Charlie, if they had their hides tanned every time you saw them it wouldn't be misplaced for if they are not coming out of an ill-turn they are going into one.'

A week after Lilly's seventy-first birthday she took ill. A feeling of weakness came over her. Charlie persuaded her to stay in bed while he walked to the doctor's surgery to ask him to call. Within half an hour, he was at the house. He examined her and had an ambulance at the door and she was taken into hospital. Charlie accompanied her and saw her into the hospital bed, but the sister told him that the doctor would soon see her to do various tests so it would be better if she were left alone until the normal visiting time. Charlie was concerned, but he did as he was bid, and made off home. He busied himself all day and returned to the hospital in the evening. The tests they had done had really tired her; she was looking very poorly and could hardly be bothered with him. It worried him so much that he telephoned Charles, and told him of the situation.

Charles came up the following day on the first available train; thankfully for Charlie he came alone. The first day of his visit, his mother was still very ill, but she was having the very best of treatment. If she had been Royalty she couldn't have had better. Charles was impressed with the hospital's high standards. The second day of his visit saw a distinct improvement. Lilly was visibly much improved, and becoming more like herself. After the hospital visit Charles caught the train home, leaving instructions with his father to ring him regularly with news on how his mother was progressing. Lilly continued to improve; the sister told Charlie they would just keep her another day or two for observation, then she could be discharged. On the Sunday evening they talked for an hour, Lilly telling him how much she was looking forward to coming home. She even walked with him as far as the hospital door.

The following morning at about seven thirty there was a policeman at Charlie's door, with instructions for Charlie to accompany him to the hospital. The doctor met them at the door, and guided Charlie into his consulting room. He sat Charlie down and told him he had dreadful news for him. Lilly had had a seizure in the night, and had died. The news hit Charlie so hard it physically stunned him. A part of his brain shut off, not allowing him to feel the full impact of what had happened. He was in a daze for weeks. Even the arrangements for the funeral, and the funeral itself, passed with him still in his numbed state. Some observers even thought him a little callous in his actions, but slowly the grief hit him, and the realisation of what he had lost came through to him. He could so easily have 'let himself go', but thankfully the discipline of his RAF days made him keep himself clean, tidy and fed.

It was several more weeks before he was able to speak to anyone on how he felt, or even to mention Lilly's name. The first time was in conversation with Fred. They were in the White Swan, and they'd each had a couple of pints of beer.

'Fred, whoever decides these sort of things could have let Lilly have a few more years. We had our ups and downs, like everybody else, but nobody knows how I miss her, and to have to die suddenly like that, and Fred, you know she never ailed a thing in her life till that terrible day. Looking back, she had been part of my life ever since I was a nipper. First off she was a school friend of our Hannah's, she was part of our household; she spent so much time with us that she called my mother Ma, same as Hannah and myself, and when we started courting she never gave me a moment's doubt, she never so much as looked off her book. Fred, it just wasn't fair.'

'When was life ever fair in this neck of the woods, I ask you, Charlie, have we ever had anything that's been fair? But Charlie, you have no reason to reproach yourself, you gave her a good life, she was happy in what she did. She enjoyed her life, and got a lot of fulfilment from it. She bore a son whom she was proud of, and she helped him to do well for himself, and, best of all, she's seen her child's children. So Charlie, me old lad, all you can do now is keep your chin up, and get on with life as best you can.'

After that conversation Charlie was able to talk about Lilly, and slowly the pain began to ease. Life carried on for him as near normal as it was ever going to be. About once a year Charlie still received a cursory visit from Charles and his family. They were visits that filled Charlie with some trepidation, for the two youngsters' behaviour had not improved. They no longer stayed overnight on their visits; it was easier all round if they stayed overnight at a local hotel, and just spent an hour or two with Charlie before continuing their journey.

Charlie was thankful, for he would never forget the last time they stayed over. Charlie's immediate next-door neighbours were Ish and May West. Poor May took a lot of ribbing, because she was exactly opposite to her namesake, the film star Mae West. May was as thin as a lath, shapeless, and as plain as a pikestaff, but they were really decent people. The two families had lived in harmony for over twenty-five years. Ish West was a keen gardener, and spent hours in his small garden; his dahlias and chrysanthemums were his pride and joy. May enjoyed cooking, and was very good with it. On her baking days she always gave Charlie a taste of everything she baked, and if they were having anything special for Sunday lunch, Charlie was invited.

On the fateful day of his grandchildren's visit they hadn't been out of his sight for five minutes when they had slipped into Ish's garden, found his clippers, cut off all of his dahlias, and rearranged them by sticking them back in the soil on the opposite side of the garden. Poor Ish was devastated. Charlie felt dreadful about it, but all he could say was how sorry he was. The rift the incident caused took nearly a year to heal. Charlie really missed the treats that he had become used to for May's cooking was a bit special.

'Hello there, Charlie, are you not coming in to see us to-day? You're standing there like you've lost a ten pound note.'

Charlie turned quickly to see young Stanley Batley grinning at him from the compound that held the new cars in Joe Williamson's Motor Complex. Stanley was a trainee salesman who had a cheeky face but who was pleasant with it. Charlie knew the youngster's father, Oily Bob Batley, who repaired old cars in a back street garage and was a regular at the White Swan.

Charlie lied to the youngster. 'I haven't time to-day, Stanley, I have to get home.'

'I'm going up the street now, I'll drop you at the top if you'd like.'

Charlie didn't want to ride in a car that day, he wanted to walk, so he had to lie again. 'I have a message to do further down the street first, but thanks for the offer.'

'Maybe another time, Charlie, then.'

'Yeh, sure thing, Stanley.'

Charlie hadn't intended going any further down the street: very few shoppers did, because Joe Williamson's Motor Complex had cut the few remaining businesses off. Anyone going further down the street was usually going for a specific purpose. Charlie, having lied to Stanley, felt obliged to carry on down the street.

CHAPTER 20

The Motor Complex seemed to go on for ever. Charlie was out of breath by the time he was past it. Looking a bit pathetic, and standing on its own, was Westwood's shop, 'sticking out like a sore thumb' crossed his mind. Printed across the window in large gold leaf lettering it boasted 'Specialists in Ladies' Gowns, and Fashions for all High Class Functions'. The shop had been there unchanged for as long as Charlie could remember. Over the years it had had the cream of society for customers: titled ladies, film stars, top sportswomen, the wives of top sportsmen and many other big names in industry and politics. Before the war, when schoolgirls dreamt of marrying their millionaires, princes, dukes, earls, or other royalty, they were all going to buy their gowns from Westwood's. Over the last few weeks the shop had been the subject of a lot of conjecture as to its future. There was a strong rumour that they were in severe financial difficulties and the business would go under very quickly. They had been unable to pay the assistant who had been with them for ten years or more, and had had to 'let her go'. From Charlie's standpoint however it didn't look to be on the verge of bankruptcy; the shop was full of expensive stock and the daughter, who was now the owner, had her nearly new top-of-the-range BMW standing at the door. The White Swan was where all the gossip was taking place, and Charlie had taken it all in.

Years ago Charlie had been a customer, yes, a customer there as well, and Lilly had been a potential one. When Charles was to be married, Lilly decided she would have a new outfit, and asked Charlie if he would accompany her to Westwood's shop to have a look, and see what they had to offer. The shop was run by mother and daughter. The mother was a Westwood; she was married to Harry Stevenson but still used the title Miss Westwood: Harry was jokingly referred to as Mr Westwood. She was near retiring age when Lilly and Charlie entered the shop, but she personally came to them to see to their needs. Lilly told her of the occasion, and what she was looking for. Lilly was good with clothes, always knew what she wanted, usually had the colours right, and always looked good in them. Miss Westwood told her she knew exactly what she wanted, and brought out a grey suit with a very faint, large overcheck in red. Charlie could see straight away that Lilly was not impressed with it, but Miss Westwood was adamant that this was the suit for her. The situation was amusing Charlie for Lilly was not a rude person, and was doing her best to keep civil with Miss Westwood in very trying circumstances. Miss Westwood was in full stride, telling Lilly how the faint red check would give her greater flexibility in her choice of hat, handbag and shoes, and was really talking down to her. Harry Stevenson was in the shop, and came over to have a word with Charlie. It was quite a warm day. Charlie was in his shirt-sleeves, but Harry had a long grey overcoat on, right down to his knees, and a scarf round his neck. He looked terrible, his complexion as grey as his overcoat. Charlie had heard that he wasn't in very good health, but didn't know he was as ill as he appeared. They hadn't been talking for five minutes when Lilly came over, ready to leave the shop. Charlie could see that she was quite boiling. Miss Westwood had the last word: 'Think on that suit, my dear, elite people with talent and flair will appreciate its merits, I can assure you on that.'

Walking up the street Lilly was not so reticent, and gave vent to her feelings. 'Charlie, did you see what that condescending, supercilious old witch tried to palm off on to me? She tried to con me like the two tricksters that sold the fairytale king the invisible suit of clothes, only the knowledgeable could see it. Charlie, the suit was frumpish, out-moded, out-dated, and monstrously over-priced. She must think I came down with the last shower of rain. It's my first time in her shop, but, believe me, it's the last. We'll go to the town tomorrow, and find something there.'

Charlie was still finding the whole episode funny, and was trying to console her and keep a straight face. Then she too began to see the funny side of it and started to smile. She gave Charlie a playful whop on the backside with her handbag, and told him, 'And you can stop patronizing me too.'

That night in the White Swan Charlie told Fred of what had happened in the shop, and mentioned how ill Harry Stevenson had looked. Fred knew more about the family, and told Charlie a bit about their history.

'It was a real top shop before the war, but it didn't change to suit the needs of modern ladies. It's been losing money for years. If it wasn't for the son-in-law the business would have been bust long ago, and you know, Charlie, even though they are losing money they still like the high life, and Miss Westwood's man Harry hasn't been any help; he's kidded everyone all his life that he is ailing. Ah knows he looks like he's "going about just saving funeral expenses", but if he would get that top coat off, and get out into the fresh air he would look different. The only thing that's wrong with him is lazyitis. Even in the war-time he wangled his way out of the Services, pretending to be sick. The doctor gave him a green card to start at the colliery, but he wangled his way out of that too; the shock at the thought of having to work made him take to the couch for three years. And do you know, Charlie, Miss Westwood will not have a wrong word said about him. The daughter Moira, she married young Raymond Hedworth, you probably know him, do you, Charlie?'

'Yes, he was brought up just two streets from us.'

'Well, Moira is anything but fair to him, he must be out of his mind for contributing to them.'

The following day Charlie and Lilly took the train into Newcastle where they were spoiled for choice. In the end, Lilly chose a matching dress and overjacket in a lovely flowing material, in soft powder blue. Even Charlie, who didn't have a lot of dress sense, could appreciate the attractiveness of the outfit.

The day before they were to leave for the wedding Lilly gave the outfit a last try on. Seeing the outfit in a different light she was disappointed to find that the soft blue of the dress made the freckles on her neck more pronounced. She said to Charlie, 'Charlie, I need something to cover my neck. When we were in Westwood's the other day I noticed they had some pleasant silk cravats on a rail at the back of the shop. One of those would be ideal. I could even use the pearl and sapphire pin my mother left me to hold it, but there's no way I'm going into that woman's shop for it.'

'I'll go for it for you,' Charlie answered.

'If you do, don't pay any more than about three pounds or so for it.'

149

So Charlie became a customer of Westwood's. As instructed by Lilly, he chose a silk cravat in pearl grey, but he didn't dare tell her that he paid over eleven pounds.

If all the stories were true, and Charlie believed them to be so because all of his information had came from reliable sources, chiefly Fred who had taken a great interest in what had been happening, Miss Westwood's daughter was having the worst time of her life. The rumours that were rife were true. She was in severe financial trouble, and unless she could raise money somehow or reunite with her husband, the clothes shop she had inherited from her mother would have to close, and she would have seriously to alter her life style.

Moira had always had the best of everything; she was an only child and many would say spoilt. Since her teens she could have any boy she wanted, for she had been a beautiful young woman, tall, slender, long-legged, shapely, and topped with an exquisite head of fair hair. Coupled with the finest clothes, she was altogether a charming young lady and had often been referred to as 'every man's dream girl'. She was well aware of her attributes, and made the most of her striking appearance. Her mother had been furious when she announced her intention to marry Raymond Hedworth: 'throwing herself away on such a pathetic young man who had little education, and who was struggling to run a tin pot business,' was her contention. After their marriage, when Ray moved into Moira's house, the house she had been left in her grandmother's will, her mother was up in arms, calling Ray all the spongers and scroungers she could lay her tongue to.

What her mother didn't know was that Moira had a pregnancy scare. It turned out to be a false alarm, but at the time she was frantic to be married. She knew plenty of very eligible young men who were keen on her, but they all shied off at the prospect of marriage. The problem had been on her mind, and through not concentrating she had run off the road in her car and crashed into a tree. The car had caught fire and Ray, who had been following in his old van, had pulled her from the burning car in a semi-conscious state. Their courtship and marriage followed quickly after that. They settled down, and two years later had a baby girl, Millicent.

Moira's mother would still not accept Ray, and slighted him at every opportunity. Her constant disparagement of Ray coloured Moira's feelings, dissatisfaction crept in, and their unsuitability began to show. Ray was engulfed in his work, leaving the house before seven each morning, long before Moira was astir, and not returning till six or seven in the evening, by which time Moira was engaged in her own pastimes. It was left to Greta, their cook cum cleaning lady, to see to his meal. It was something Greta enjoyed, and she would stay till any hour, without extra money, to see to Ray's dinner. Moira constantly complained that Ray had no social aspirations whatsoever: even on Sunday, his only day off, he was content to job around the house and garden, whereas Moira, with her mother's encouragement, looked for more out of life.

They had a nanny for Millicent for her first five years, and then started her at a private school near Moira's mother's house. This meant she spent a lot of her free time with her. Nearly every evening it was left to Ray to see her to bed.

The shop wasn't a problem to Moira; she had an assistant employed and her mother was usually in attendance. Money wasn't a problem either, for despite her mother's disparaging remarks about Ray, he did pay his share. They had a joint personal account at the bank, and this was a big help to her. When she needed large sums of extra money to finance her expensive pastimes it was easy to remortgage her house or shop. Her activities were expensive. She tried several, but eventually settled on tournament golf and competition ball-room dancing. Ray was quite a good dancer, but he was just an inch or two too short for her; to have danced with him she'd have had to wear lower heels, but with the gowns she wore she wouldn't be seen dead in low heels. It wasn't a problem; she was never short of a partner. Reginald Newton, a family friend, was one of her favourites, but by no means her only partner. She'd have married Reginald, heaven knows they had courted long enough, but when Moira was desperate for a husband Reginald had decided to stay on at university and study the classics. It was one of her mother's great disappointments that she and Reginald hadn't married.

Of course to be part of the competition golf and dancing scene it was necessary to have a large expensive car which had to be changed regularly, coupled with the necessary tuition. It was altogether very expensive, but Moira didn't have any trouble meeting the costs.

The first real sign of Ray's discontent had been at Moira's aunt's ruby wedding party. They were all invited. Because there would be lots of drink, Moira asked Ray to drive them with her mother and father to the party. Moira's mother didn't like Ray to drive her car, or for that matter even ride in it, so they travelled in Ray's old car. She hadn't turned her back on him for more than five minutes when he had slipped out of her aunt's house and driven back to his mother's. His mother, a widow, had died about six months previously and had left Ray her small terraced house. Moira knew that Ray had had a good offer for the house, and didn't know why he hadn't accepted it.

Moira was furious with him, but as the days passed, and he didn't come home, her fury gradually turned to bewilderment. Her mother was delighted. 'Best place for him, the snivelling weed,' she said, but Moira was beginning to miss him, realising that he had been a sort of comfort to her. With hindsight, she should have seen a change in him, but he was a bit like a poker player: he didn't show much emotion, making his attitude hard to fathom. Not, she had to admit, that she had tried much, at least not in the past, but now she was looking at the situation with different eyes. She raked her mind for the main pointers as to what had gone wrong.

On their daughter's fifth birthday, Moira's mother asked if she could arrange a party for the child, but what an embarrassment it had been for Ray. At the time it had annoyed Moira, and she hadn't even been on the receiving end. She had really felt for him. Mother had been in fine form. She had invited all of Moira's friends, several of them ex-boyfriends, and had proceeded to show Ray up at every opportunity. For their tea everyone was given fine china cups, all except Ray who was given a thick chalky mug. Every chance she had she had made remarks like, 'What sort of a sponger marries a girl just to have the good life, and, mind you, moves into her house.' At the time Ray never said a word, but he had never again set foot in her mother's house.

Then there was the incident over the holiday they were to have in the Bahamas. Moira was going to pay for it from money she had been left in an aunt's will. Ray had cried off at the last minute, so she had taken her mother and father in his place. On their return Ray had been even quieter than usual. Looking back, she should have made an effort and taken the trouble to look closer at the affair, but she had just let it pass.

He had embarrassed her in front of a vet friend of hers, Nigel Watts, who had been a friend of the family for years; she often played golf with him. Just a couple of years after Millicent had been born, she had fancied going into show-jumping. They had acquired Gordon, a good horse and expensive, with a good record in the show ring. The sport wasn't for her, and after her first mishap when she had fallen from him, she had told Ray he should be sold. Ray had found a farm, well out of town, to board the horse until a buyer could be found. She had almost forgotten him, until one day she had a telephone call from the farmer, saying that Gordon had had an accident. A dog had run him into some barbed wire, and he was badly hurt. She had telephoned Nigel who had looked at the horse, then called at the house. Between them they had decided, taking into account his age and his injuries, and the fact that the boy whose dog had done the damage didn't have money to meet the cost of the treatment, that the best course of action would be to have Gordon 'put to sleep'. Ray had came in at the last minute, had ignored her wishes, then been positively rude to Nigel. He had called another vet who spent all night on Gordon, costing a fortune, though she had to admit he did save him, and as far as she knew Gordon was still going strong.

Then there was their daughter's wedding. It had been held in a top hotel and had cost Ray the most of £7,000. The day before the ceremony Ray had quietly announced that he wouldn't be attending. He wouldn't give a reason, and for a while Moira had had a bad feeling about it, but as there was so much to do she didn't have time to dwell on it. Mother had of course been delighted and, looking back, Millicent hadn't been much bothered either. It had now been over a year since their marriage, and Ray had never even mentioned their names.

It was about three weeks after Ray had left, when she had the first inkling of her financial difficulties. The bank bounced two of her cheques, both of them from their joint personal account. One was for £820, the subscription to one of her golf clubs, the other for £1,900 which she had paid to the Local Authority as rates for her shop.

She rang Jack Hastings who worked in the bank; he was a friend from the Golf Club, and always looked after her in her bank dealings. He promised to look into it, and call her back. This he did within five minutes, with the information that no funds had been transferred to the account, and there was nothing more he could do; she would have to see the manager. She made an appointment for the following day. Her mother accompanied her and they had never been so humiliated in their lives.

Their visit to the bank didn't last five minutes. The manager told them that because of the shop's financial record there was no way he could loan any money, and when she suggested mortgaging her house or shop, he had laughed and told them they were living in 'Fantasy Land'. In a last attempt to raise money, a last 'throw of the dice' as it were, Moira gave him a quick synopsis of what had happened, a pleading look on her face and a crocodile tear in her eye. It worked with most of the men she knew, but not with the bank manager. He simply said, 'You've thrown your bucket down the well without the rope being attached, haven't you?', and closed the door on them.

They were both angered, but powerless to do anything about it. Even though her mother had been in on what the bank manager had said, she would not accept how bad the situation was. She still believed they had a top shop and that money somehow would become available.

Every Thursday she had been in the habit of calling at 'the hole in the wall', using her bank card to draw the money to pay Cathy, her shop-assistant, her mother for her efforts in the shop, and Greta her cook cum cleaner. Her card was limited as to how much she could draw, so she always took the maximum on Thursdays and would call again on Fridays to make up the difference. She put the card in the machine, and a notice immediately flashed on the screen: 'Card withheld, refer to bank.' She had forgotten that the card drew money from their joint personal account, and that that source of money had dried up. She was devastated, drove to the shop and looked in the till, but there wasn't enough to pay for her hair appointment. Her legs had turned to jelly. She didn't know what she would do without her bank card, it was a major part of her life; she had always used it not only for paying wages but also for petrol, car servicing, and all the incidental expenses incurred by her other interests, such as her stopovers at the various hotels where golf and dancing tournaments were held. Then another fact dawned on her. She couldn't pay the week's wages. She would have to tell Cathy and Greta that she could no longer afford their services, and that she could not pay them for this week. She would promise them that if she could sort out her finances she would settle with them.

Cathy burst into tears when she was told, and ran off home without a word. Greta was a different kettle of fish; she fair lashed into Moira, bawling her out like a fish wife, with a few choice expletives thrown in.

'Here's a few home truths for you, Madam,' she said. 'I don't need your money. I've a feeling you'll need it more than me; you're a lazy, useless, spoilt, extravagant trollop, and I wouldn't be here at all if it hadn't been that I feel for Ray. The way you and that lump you call a mother treat him is disgusting.'

While she was lambasting Moira, Greta was pulling on her coat and hat and making for the door. Moira was dumbfounded, and stood with her mouth open. Half-way through the door, Greta delivered her last shot:

'I hear Ray has found someone else. I hope its true, and I hope he finds a bit of happiness with her and a bit of respect, 'cos it's something he's never had with you. He's always had the "claggy end of the stick" with you lot. One thing's for sure: whatever he's doing he's better off than with a slut like you.'

In her whole life Moira had never been spoken to like that. All types of emotion bubbled up in her: anger, frustration, nervousness, everything, she wanted to strike back, but what could she do? If she called the police they would be unsympathetic; Greta had worked a week and had no prospects of being paid. She thought of consulting a solicitor, but a lot of what Greta had said was true, and she certainly wouldn't like the revelations made public. It was true she had had a few indiscretions. Some of the golf and dancing tournaments she attended were held in top hotels and usually required a stop-over; they were romantic events and some of the men were 'stunners', real good looking and keen on her. She had not always said no! She decided it was better just to try and forget what Greta had said. She lay awake most of the night, and when events cleared slightly in her mind, what troubled her most was Greta's last statement on Ray seeing another woman. By the end of the night she came to the conclusion it couldn't be true. It was just spite on Greta's part. It wasn't possible that unassuming Ray would choose another woman in preference to her.

Moira's Aunt May's ruby wedding party had been the last straw for Ray. Moira asked him to drive herself, her mother and her father to the party. May was one of the very few of Moira's family to treat him with any sort of normality, and he quite liked her for it. He would attend her celebrations.

'We will take your car,' Moira said, 'it will be better.'

Ray knew what was behind that statement. He knew her mother didn't like him driving her car. 'Better for her is what you mean,' he thought to himself. He drove them there, and when they were settled Aunt May came over and spent a little time with him. She couldn't stay with him for long; it would have been rude to ignore her other guests.

'What would you like to drink?' she had said to him after their conversation.

'It will have to be something light, I have to drive home later.'

'I have some really nice non-alcoholic wine, will you have a glass of that?'

'Yes, that will do fine.'

She poured Ray a generous glass, and left him while she mingled with her other guests. He had no sooner sat down with the drink when Moira, her mother and father came to him separately, each with the same statement: 'I hope you haven't forgotten that you are driving home, so do go easy on the drink.' Ray's temper was rising as he gave them all the same answer: 'It's a non-alcoholic drink.' They were making it seem that he was in the habit of drinking and driving. It wouldn't have hurt so much, if he had not had strong views on the subject: it was something he abhorred, and would never do.

He turned to some of the family on his right, in an effort to join in the conversation. They ignored him, and gave him the cold shoulder. He turned to the right to speak to two of Moira's cousins. One of them deliberately turned her chair so her back was to him. He knew what it was, Moira's mother had poisoned them to him with her malicious tongue. Reginald Newton walked into the room; he seemed to turn up at all of Moira's family events. He walked over to Moira and put his arm round her waist; they put their heads together and, laughing and giggling, walked out into the garden. In the past Ray would have shrugged his shoulders and stood this sort of behaviour, but this time he couldn't take it. He quietly put down his non-alcoholic drink. He walked into the hall where May had just welcomed a guest, took her to one side and told her, 'May, I'm sorry but I'm afraid there's reasons why I'm going to have to leave your party. I can't explain at the minute, but I hope you'll understand.'

'Don't try, lad, I know what you are feeling.' She reached up and kissed him on the cheek. 'Good luck to you, lad.'

Ray picked up his jacket and, without another word to anyone, drove home to the house his mother had left him.

Ray had not had the easiest of lives. He had left school at fifteen, when the only job he could find was assistant to Bert Telford, a fruit and vegetable salesman who supplied a few small shops and ran a barrow in surrounding towns, usually on their market days. Ray learned a lot about the fruit and vegetable business from Bert, and when he was old enough he was taught to drive the van. Shortly after that Bert's health failed him. He lay for several weeks, terribly ill, and in that time Ray ran the business. Bert never recovered from his illness, and when he died Mrs Telford asked Ray to call round. She told him that Bert had thought highly of him, and that it was his wish for Ray to have the business, on condition that he pay his widow £500 within a year. There wasn't much to the business, just the old van and the barrow, but Ray was delighted and readily agreed to the terms. He didn't want to change the name of the business, as he didn't want to spoil the good contacts and reputation that had been made. Mrs Telford had no hesitation in allowing Ray to use the title 'Telford's Fruit and Vegetables'. Ray worked very hard and was soon able to pay the money to Mrs Telford.

Then he started making changes. He sold the barrow, as he had no wish to stand on the streets selling fruit and vegetables. He then dropped 'Fruit and Vegetables' from the title and renamed the business just 'Telford's'. He branched out into other food lines, including frozen foods. He found a very profitable niche in the market, and the business boomed. Within two years the turnover rocketed as did the profits. In the same two years he acquired new premises, thirty employees and a fleet of vehicles. Fortune was certainly with him.

The only black spot had been his misfortune in following Moira Stevenson in his old van when she ran off the road. It was the unluckiest day of his life when he pulled her semi-conscious from her burning car. What she saw in him Ray never knew. He had never been any sort of a heart-throb, no girl had ever gone out of her way to know him, yet Moira had pestered the life out of him till he eventually agreed to marry her. It had been a big mistake on his part. On her insistence he had moved into her house, though he could easily have bought a house for them, but Moira wouldn't hear of it.

After a few weeks she changed abruptly. He found she had no interest in him or his work. To make matters worse, for some reason her mother hated him: why he didn't know, he hadn't done anything to hurt either her or Moira. She berated him at every opportunity. She openly called him a sponger and scrounger, because he had moved into Moira's house. It just wasn't true. He paid far more than his share, in fact he paid all the expenses. Moira and he had a joint personal account. It was very one sided: he paid into it and she spent from it. Some months he had to transfer thousands of pounds to keep the account running. His bank manager and accountant were both concerned about it, but to keep the peace he kept it up.

Their daughter Millicent had been subject to too much influence from Moira's mother, and to sum up their daughter's character, she was a spoiled brat. After what she had done just previous to her marriage, if he never saw her again, he wouldn't shed tears. Ray knew Moira was cheating on him on her weekends away; there were plenty only too pleased to 'whisper in his ear', and tell him what was going on. He was beyond it bothering him. It would have pleased him if she would have stayed away, but she never did. All he ever heard at home was Lady this or Lady That, the latest 'big name' to visit the shop, or about the next golf or dancing competition. Ray could have been interested if they could have been discussed reasonably, but on and on about the same subjects was more than he could take. His needs or wants were never considered. All he could do to keep himself sane was to bury himself in his work.

One of Moira's aunts died and left her five thousand pounds in her will. The morning she received the money, it was a Saturday and Ray was at home. Moira was excited with the windfall, and invited Ray to go on holiday with her. 'We'll go to the travel agent and book two or three weeks in the Bahamas; we'll have the holiday of a life-time!' she said. At first Ray had been sceptical about the idea, thinking she could have put the money to better use, as her shop was ailing, and in need of funds. Then the idea grew on him: he was after all subsidising the shop, so he wasn't actually taking anything from her by taking the holiday with her. He had never had a holiday in his life, and two weeks before they were to go he was really looking forward to it. He had one of the brochures the travel agent had given him in his office at work; he marvelled at the luxury of it all, the hotel and its grounds, the beaches and the palm trees. He had everything arranged. Joyce Rowntree, his assistant, whom he would trust with his life, would look after the business for him, and he was all set to go.

That evening, when he returned home, the whole bottom of his world was knocked out. Moira was on the telephone, and didn't hear him coming into the house. He could only hear Moira's side of the conversation, but it didn't take him long to understand what it was all about. It was the holiday that was being discussed. '. . . there's ructions on, Mother thinks that as the money came from our side of the family it should only benefit my aunt's immediate family; to put it bluntly she thinks I should take her and Dad.'

There was a pause as the other party spoke.

'. . . and she thinks Ray is too dumb to appreciate it. I have to agree I've been a bit hasty inviting Ray, and I've rued . . .'

Again there was a pause.

'. . . besides, the sunshine will do Dad the power of good. We've been to see the travel agent to-day, and providing we make the changes in the next few days, the booking can be altered. I'm not looking forward to telling Ray, I think he's actually looking forward to it, but I ask you, what else can I do to keep the peace?'

Ray had heard enough. He slipped quietly out of the house, and came in again with a clash of the door. The following morning he made his excuses, and saved her the embarrassment of telling him. He was mad at what had been done to him. It wasn't as if her mother and father hadn't had a holiday; they were off on a regular basis, probably, if the truth were known, funded by Ray.

He had been thinking for a long time that the situation for him was untenable. There had to be something better in life for him. He actually said out loud to himself, 'There can't be anything worse.' While they were away on the holiday, which was for seventeen days, he took the first positive steps towards getting him off the treadmill. A big national company had been interested for quite some time in taking over his business. The situation had posed a dilemma for him: the company was desperate to have a foothold in the region, and he wasn't such a fool as not to know that if they set up in opposition to him it would have a disastrous effect. His personal problems gave him the impetus to make his move.

He had the shock of his life when, at the end of the deal, he had £1.7 million pounds, mostly in company shares in the bank, shares that had already increased in value by nearly £60,000. He also had a well paid job with the company. He and Joyce Rowntree were joint managers for the northern part of the business. It was a reasonable job, but it didn't carry the worries that had been on his shoulders in the years he had spent building the business up. He no longer had the burden of keeping it financially viable. With these worries off his mind, he had time to reflect on his life, and he didn't like what he was seeing. In all his life he had never been a quitter, and he didn't like the idea of giving up on his marriage, but he knew that he was at the end of his tether, he had had enough. It couldn't go on. For twenty-four years he had been made a fool of. He studied his situation and thought of trying to talk it out with Moira, but knew it was hopeless, she was too dyed in the wool to change. His only hope of any sort of a life would be when his marriage was over.

A few weeks after the holiday, Ray came home from work to find Moira had a visitor. It was Nigel Watts, a long time friend of Moira's family and he was a vet by profession. Ray couldn't stand him, but he looked into the sitting room and spoke to them before he carried on through to the dining room, where as usual Greta served him his dinner. He could hear the mumble of their conversation, punctuated by Nigel's deep, penetrating laugh. Ray's temper was rising. The laugh was reminding him of the last time he had been in Moira's mother's house. She had given a party for his daughter's fifth birthday, which had been just a ruse to do everything she could do to humiliate Ray. He had nearly finished his dinner, and Moira and Nigel were still talking, but getting near to the door.

'What's he here for?' he asked Greta.

'Something about Gordon, her horse; he's had some sort of an accident. He's hurt bad, and from what I can make of the conversation they're going to have to put him down.'

Ray rose quickly from the table and hurried to the door. He ignored Nigel and addressed Moira, with thunder on his face.

'What's happening?'

'It's old Gordon, he's been chased by a young boy's dog, and he got himself tangled up in some barbed wire. He's so badly hurt and considering his age, Nigel and I have decided that the best thing to do is to have him put to sleep.'

It was plain for both of them to see Ray was livid.

'The pair of you have a nerve, haven't you? The horse is not yours, it's mine, I don't believe you can think on how many years it is since you set eyes on him and one thing's for sure, neither you nor he will make any decision about him.'

Nigel spoke up. 'Look here, now, I was called by Moira to look at the horse, and I've given my professional opinion: he should be put down, he's suffering badly.'

'But not suffering so much that you can't spend at least half an hour here gassing. I think nothing of your opinion, so I'll get a second one. You just take yourself off and forget about the horse, and don't worry, you'll be paid, just send me your bill. Now get out of my sight till I find someone more capable to see to Gordon.'

Ray stood for a few seconds, his eyes dark with fury, but neither Moira nor Nigel dared say a word to him. They each turned their backs and went their separate ways.

Ray rang Mr Groves, the farmer who looked after Gordon for him, and asked if Mr Hastings, the vet he had seen at work on the farm, would look at Gordon. Mr Groves agreed, and said he'd ring him. He explained quickly how Gordon had had the accident, and that he had rung the house for permission to call Mr Hastings, but Moira had insisted that Nigel call to see the horse. From the conversation Ray gathered the farmer was less than impressed by Nigel. Although Ray had never been on a horse's back in his life, Gordon was special to him. He had paid £3,000 for him, when Moira had a fad to take up showjumping; the craze hadn't lasted long and Ray had been left with the horse. He really should have been sold as money was tight for him at the time. He found temporary stabling for him with the Groves family of Throstles Nest Farm, with the intention of finding a buyer. It never happened, as the Groves family were so genuine and accommodating, and so good to Gordon, that Ray hadn't the heart to take him away. Wendy their daughter was the one who did the most to his upkeep. Ray didn't know much about horses, but the girl he had bought him from had given him a good tip on what to look for to see if a horse had been cared for:

'Look no further than a horse's fore legs to see if he has been abused at all. Run your hands down his fore legs; they should be clean in every way, and his hooves should be tidy and look right.'

'What do you mean by his legs being clean?'

'They should be free of any lumps, bumps, swellings or sores.'

Every fourth Saturday afternoon Ray had made the trip up to the farm to pay for Gordon's keep. It was about half an hour's drive, situated right on the edge of the moors. Wendy always insisted he saw Gordon, and he couldn't help but notice that the horse's legs were as clean as the day he had bought him. It would have been a shame to waste such a good horse, so Ray had given his permission for Wendy to ride him in local gymkhanas. She had done so well on him that she now had sponsorship, and rode for one of the big stables. Gordon was too old now for eventing, but he was still well looked after, and Wendy still rode him gently over the moors for exercise.

Ray and Mr Groves had had many a friendly argument over the payment of Gordon's keep. As Wendy had sole use of Gordon, Mr Groves would have kept him for nothing or at the most half the going rate for a horse's keep, but Ray would have none of it. He always insisted on paying the full rate. Looking at in cold, monetary terms, it looked as if Ray had the worst of the bargain, but he gained in other ways. When he called every fourth Saturday afternoon, he was always given a cup of tea before being shown the horse. He would then take half an hour to walk over the field, then back to the farm through a small wood and alongside a stream. It was so tranquil there that he found solace, comfort and inspiration, something he never found at home with Moira. There he was able to make a lot of decisions regarding both his business and his private life. He was by no means emotionally attached to Gordon, but he was important to him because of the other benefits that came with him.

Ray put his coat on, and drove up to the farm. Mr Hastings had arrived just a few minutes before him and had assessed the situation. Mr Groves had cut most of the wire away and had Gordon in a loose box. Mr Hastings was doing all the talking.

'I've examined him; all of his injuries are bad, but I can deal with them all. The trouble is, like all animals he's a bit petty. I cannot promise that after all the work it will take, he won't up and die on us, but I'm willing to treat him for you if you will allow me.'

He was looking at Ray, who nodded his consent. He then spoke to Mr Groves.

'Ring my surgery for me and ask my assistant to come over, and bring all the hands you can till we get him put under.' Mr Groves left on his errand, and the vet kept on talking. 'I'm going to inject him now with a massive dose of penicillin, and then another jab to eliminate the risk of lockjaw. I have a new anaesthetic, one injection and he's out, and then when we are finished, an injection of the antidote and he's back round again. Its a wonderful innovation; in fact without it I wouldn't like to tackle this operation.'

Mr Groves returned, with his family, just his wife and Wendy, who were all the hands he could muster.

'Most of his injuries are on his right hand side. When I give him this injection he'll totter round for a bit, so I want everybody to be ready, and make sure he goes down on his left side.'

It happened exactly how the vet had explained. Gordon was guided to the centre of the box and when the horse started to lose consciousness, he was steadied down on his left side.

Mr Hastings' assistant arrived, and they both worked for hours on Gordon. He had many injuries, the worst one being to his hip, where the wire had cut right through the flesh and into the bone. It was after midnight before the final stitches were put in, but they had made a marvellous job. Mr Hastings was exhausted when the operation was over, and as he cleaned himself up in preparation to go home, his parting words were:

'We've done the best we can. I'll be back to-morrow to have a look at him. The next forty-eight hours will be the telling time for him.'

He then gave Gordon an injection of the antidote. Gordon stirred and tried to raise his head.

'We'll put the lights out now, and leave him in peace.'

Gordon survived, and soon returned to his usual self. The vet's bill was over £600, which Ray was happy to pay, plus £30 for Nigel Watts, which he also paid, albeit grudgingly.

Two months or so later, one of Moira's friends called on her, Ray didn't catch her surname, he only knew her as Ruth. She was one of the better mannered friends and she insisted on including Ray in the conversation. The opening gambit ruffled Ray's feathers. Ruth had no sooner sat down when she said to Moira, 'I was sorry to hear about the accident to your horse.'

As quick as lightning, Moira replied, 'Yes, it was a terrible affair, he had horrendous injuries. The vet's bill was a positive arm and a leg, but he's such an old sweetie I was only too pleased to pay for him.'

Ray boiled but said nothing. She had not even set eyes on him for at least the last fourteen years, hadn't even bothered going to see him after he had recovered. Then the purpose of Ruth's visit came into the conversation. She had lost her husband eight months previously and was still grieving for him. She was in a dilemma. There was a chap she cared about, and who was keen on her. She needed someone to talk to and to give their opinions, and advise her. Moira's answer to her problems sent all the alarm bells ringing in Ray's head:

'If I were in your position I wouldn't hesitate for five minutes; I'd be married again before you could say Jack Robinson.'

Ray was the youngest of three of a family. His father, elder brother and sister had all died in their late forties or early fifties. Ray was under no illusions; his chances of making 'old bones' were very slim. He had never spared himself, had always worked, and had never been frightened to take 'the heavy end'. The type of man that Moira admired was cagey, workshy, very guarded against any commitment, cautious of marriage, and fond of the 'good life'. But if she had her hands on Ray's £1.7 million it would probably be a different story. The thoughts of any of them languishing in luxury on the strength of his money nauseated him. Ray had never been able to fathom why this type of man was admired by Moira's family. They were all from the same mould, tall, dark, handsome he had to admit, and all with the gift of the gab. Bert Telford, Ray's ex-employer, had a description for the likes of them: 'like the big white horse, great looker, but won't yoke.' Reginald Newton, an ex-boyfriend: he'd milked the education system till he was well into his thirties, and even now, after all his education, was just something in leisure in the Town Hall. Nigel Watts, another great family friend, had studied and come out as a vet but when called to look at Gordon would take the easy way out and send for the knackerman, instead of taking his coat off and buckling down to what needed to be done. Yet these were the type who were held in high regard, and Moira's father, who had never lifted a finger at anything all the time Ray had known him, was positively revered. Ray, who had never done wrong to any of them, was barely tolerated by Moira and her family, and was despised by her mother.

It wasn't too hard a decision: Ray wanted out of the sham of a marriage. He confided his fears to his accountant and bank manager, not really expecting them to take his situation too seriously, but he couldn't have been more wrong. They liaised with each other and came up with the solution that would make sure neither Moira nor any of her family laid hands on any of his money.

The accountant told him, 'It's not really the done thing for me to advise you on what to do, but I will put you in touch with someone who can. It will cost you a fair amount of money, but I think you'll find it'll be worth it.'

Within a week Ray had his consultation, and the expert's advice acted on. Nearly all his money and shares were deposited in a Swiss bank, who were to take care of all his financial worries. They would make sure his capital and shares were made the best of, and he made a will leaving it all to his as yet unborn grandchildren, thinking that by missing a generation, he could be sure there'd be no more influence from Moira's mother. If there were to be no grandchildren, his money was to go to the local hospital.

Ray had no sooner settled his financial worries, when a further complication entered his life. Rosemary Edwards, a friend from his teenage days, called at his office to see him. He hadn't seen her for twenty-six years yet recognised her immediately. Ray was really pleased to see her. They had both been members of the local Cycling Club, and had seen quite a lot of each other for a couple of years or so, and in that time had become good friends. The Club had an active social side to it, and had held regular dances and social evenings. Rosemary and Ray had often been partners at these events. Unfortunately the Secretary of the Club had died suddenly. He had been its mainstay, so it had soon faded into obscurity, and Rosemary and Ray had lost touch. They talked for an hour or more in Ray's office, and caught up on each other's lives.

Rosemary had married a Scotsman, and had lived all her married life in Scotland. She was now a widow, having nursed her husband for four years before he eventually died. She still lived in Scotland, and was only down to Barnforth for a relative's funeral. She was to catch the train home at three o'clock that afternoon. Ray invited her to lunch, which she readily accepted. He took her to the Highways Hotel, about three miles out of town, a lovely place in attractive surroundings. They carried on their conversation and the time fairly galloped by. It came to coffee time, and an apprehensive feeling swept over him. It was only momentary as he soon fathomed out what it was. If it had been Moira he'd been with, this was the point when she would have had to 'have a word' with someone or other. Ray would have been left twiddling his thumbs while Moira balanced her coffee cup 'society style', and laughed and giggled while she talked with the President of the Chamber of Trade, the Secretary of some Golf Club, or the Chairman of some organisation or other. There was no such behaviour from Rosemary, Ray had her undivided attention throughout the afternoon.

All too soon it was time to take her to the station for the train home. They sat and talked for a while on a bench waiting for the train. As the train approached Rosemary looked at him, her head tilted to one side, her eyes looking directly into his. It was an invitation to a kiss good-bye that Ray couldn't resist. The train was only stopped for seconds, and she was gone, but it was as if his eyes had been the lens and shutter of an expensive camera. Her image sitting on the station bench was indelibly printed in his mind. Not that Rosemary was any great beauty, more the Mona Lisa type, came to Ray's mind. In fact in the beauty stakes, she probably wasn't in the same league as Moira, but she had certainly got through to Ray.

The following morning Ray had his usual meeting with Joyce Rowntree, his co-manager. Joyce had always been able to read him and she could always pick up on his moods. That morning was no exception.

'What's wrong with you this morning?'

'Nothing.'

'Don't try to kid me.'

'All right, I admit I'm hurting.'

'See the doctor, then.'

'It's not that sort of hurt.'

'The woman who called to see you yesterday?'

Ray nodded.

'We'll say no more then.'

After walking out on the ruby wedding party, Ray had kept in touch with Rosemary. He told her of what was happening in his life, and when she invited him up to Scotland for a week-end he was only too pleased to accept. Ray had his first holiday, three days in Glasgow. It was wonderful; Rosemary knew the city like the back of her hand. It was only planned for him to stay the week-end, but there was so much to see, and they got on so well together, that they stretched the week-end to three days. On returning Ray knew in his bones that the situation he was in couldn't go on. He told Joyce about his week-end in Glasgow with Rosemary, and the turmoil his life was in.

'I want things out in the open, Joyce. I want my life tidying up.'

'You mean you want Moira to know about Rosemary?'

'Yes.'

'There's a quarter I would just have to drop a word to and it would be in Miss Westwood's ear before you could blink your eye, and I don't think it would be long before it was passed on to Moira. I'll do that for you if you want me to.' Then she laughed and said, 'I wouldn't like to be in your shoes when she hears about it.'

'Do it, Joyce, it's not possible for life to become any more miserable.'

Joyce's ploy had the desired effect. At seven o'clock that evening Moira had a visit from her mother, passing on what she had heard, a triumphant smirk on her face.

'Get your coat on, Moira, we'll go straight round there and put things to rights with that cheating rubbish of a husband of yours. I always knew he would never be of any use to you.'

Moira looked in the mirror prior to leaving. She had aged by ten years in the short time Ray had been gone. They climbed into the car, but the 'low fuel' indicator wouldn't go out. When Ray had been with her this had never been a problem; she would have passed over her card and filled the tank. Now she had the embarrassment of searching through her hand-bag for her last three pounds, hardly enough to cover the bottom of the tank with petrol.

Ray for his part knew they would come. He put on his new suit, best shirt and tie, and was actually looking forward to the confrontation that he knew was inevitable. The feeling somehow surprised him, for he had always felt in awe of Moira and her family, some sort of dread of them, a distinct inferiority feeling, but he was now seeing them in a different light. When the knock came to the door, he knew who it was before he opened it, and it was no surprise to find Moira and his mother-in-law on his doorstep. Moira was taken aback at how well Ray looked, and was lost for words: not so her mother.

'We'll not beat about the bush: we've heard some disturbing stories about you, and we've come to see if they are true.'

'There's no need to stand on the doorstep, do come in.'

They came in, and the three of them stood round the sitting room table. His mother-in-law carried on where she had left off.

'We've heard you've been running around with some woman or other; in fact we've heard that you've stayed over-night at her house. Is it true?'

Ray didn't waste his breath telling them the truth, that his stay with Rosemary had been perfectly innocent; they wouldn't have believed him. 'Not strictly true. I stayed at her house for three days.'

Ray thought his mother-in-law was going into a convulsion, as she struggled for words to lambast Ray with.

'You've a despicable streak in you, you're nothing of a man, the way you walked out on our Moira at that party, showing us up the way you did, and not a word to any one. But if you think that you and that floosie that you have picked up are having any part of our Moira's house or shop, you have another think coming.'

'You want to know why I walked out? I'll tell you. I'd had enough of your selfish, greedy, mean, mercenary ways. I couldn't take any more of it. I don't know what you mean by a floosie, but if you mean someone who is normal, caring, and warm-hearted, then I suppose Rosemary is a floosie.'

Ray's quiet confidence and ready admission had them silenced and open mouthed. And Ray was far from finished with them. Looking directly at his mother-in-law, he pressed home his advantage.

'As for Moira's house and shop, I'm going to show you some copies of some papers; they'll show you that the house and shop belong to me. Your business hasn't made a brass farthing for donkey's years, and don't take my word for it, ask your bank or your accountant. So who in their right mind would loan you money with a financial record like that? All these mortgages you've been taking out have all been done in my name. I've had all the repayments to make. I've paid the full market price for the shop, and I've paid the full market price for the house twice over.'

Ray showed them the relevant papers. It was as if they had been struck dumb, but still Ray wasn't finished with them, and still his eyes didn't leave his mother-in-law.

'Your precious car, the one I haven't to touch, who do you think that belongs to? There's the invoice for it, look at it, and you'll see my name on it. Yes, it's mine, and look how much it was, within a whisker of £40,000. Your business couldn't pay for it in a month of Sundays, no, my "tin-pot" business had to.'

Moira's mother was raging, and blustering to get words out. Ray knew what was coming, but was one step ahead. 'Oh, go on, tell me again about all these big names you have for customers, but then just have a little think, and tell me what good they are to you? What do they do? Buy a frock off you once a year, or maybe every other year, that they might or might not pay for!'

They were beaten; there was nothing more they could say. His mother-in-law was still raging. Ray was saddened slightly, for Moira had tears in her eyes. His mother-in-law was first to speak.

'Come on, Moira, we'll go home, we're not listening to any more of this.'

'Yes,' said Ray. 'But just before you go, answer me this. Were you behind our Millicent's behaviour just before her wedding?'

Ray's eyes were still directed at his mother-in-law.

'I don't know what you are talking about; come on, Moira, it's time to go home.'

Under Ray's stare she became flustered and red-cheeked; she was obviously lying. Moira refused to move, and spoke for the first time.

'Just what did they do to you?'

'Nothing to me, it was to my mother. Neither of you knew her, she was a hard working, independent woman, who wouldn't take a penny from me or anyone else to help her out. Quite unlike some parasites I could mention. In all the years we have been married, I can count on one hand the number of times you have seen her, this part of the town being too down-market for you. I tried all ways to try and help her, but she would have none of it, she wouldn't take a penny from me. I would have loved to have made life easier for her. In desperation I made a deal with Edwin the coalman. If she ordered say three bags, he would deliver six, and I would pay the difference. She even twigged that ruse; poor Edwin had to lie to her and say he had a bad back and could only carry half bags. But enough of that, back to Millicent. Unbeknown to me, my mother saved for weeks and bought her a really nice tea-pot for a wedding present. They took it back to her when she was practically on her death bed, and told her it wasn't on their wedding present list. I was ashamed of her. I have a lump in my throat still over it, and I have neighbours who still will not speak to me because of it. I'll never forgive her for it, and she'll never get another thing from me.'

'I'm so sorry,' Moira said, 'I didn't know anything about that.'

'No, I don't suppose you did,' he said, but looking directly at her mother, he added, 'But she did, the whole thing had her mark all over it.'

By her reactions, Ray knew he had hit the truth; she couldn't get out of the door quickly enough, practically dragging Moira with her. She carried on her ranting on the pavement.

'Moira, we'll go and see a solicitor to-morrow. We'll make that cheating, snivelling, damned upstart sit up and take notice, see if we don't.'

The tears were rolling down Moira's face as she rounded on her mother. 'Mother, will you shut up, just this once, shut up. I'm ashamed of what I have done to him, and I'm going to do all I can to get him back.'

She had feelings she had never experienced in her life before. It wasn't till she had lain awake for hours that the awful truth dawned on her. She was jealous, jealous of Rosemary, a woman she had never met but nevertheless who caused her the most miserable night of her life, and the longest. By the end of that long, sleepless night she knew she was facing the biggest struggle of her life, and she knew that she would be very lucky to win. It wasn't difficult to tell Ray was very fond of Rosemary.

The stage was set, the stories and the rumours would be rife. Would Westwood's survive? Could Moira save her marriage? Charlie, like everyone else, would listen to all the angles. Sadly, poor Fred, who had great interest in what was going on, would never know the outcome.

CHAPTER 21

Charlie turned to make his way up the street, and home. He came face to face with Gerry Parker. He was the undertaker, and was standing outside his premises. He was still in his full regalia from conducting Fred's funeral. Charlie knew him well. He and his son ran the business. They no longer called themselves undertakers; they were now funeral directors. They were well suited to their profession. Charlie had never seen a smile on either of their faces in his life.

'Good-day to you, Charlie,' Gerry said. 'It's a sad day, you've lost a good friend today, but the main thing is, how are you?'

Charlie thought he detected a glint in Gerry's eyes, weighing him up as a potential customer.

'Yes, it's a sad day, but I'm fine, thank you, Gerry.'

Charlie gave himself a mental shake, and quickened his stride up the street . . .